FOR MOM and Dad
—Mike

Hippo Park

An imprint of Astra Books for Young Readers,
a division of Astra Publishing House
astrapublishinghouse.com
Printed in China

ISBN: 978-1-6626-4018-6 (hc)
ISBN: 978-1-6626-4019-3 (pb)
ISBN: 978-1-6626-4020-9 (eBook)
Library of Congress Control Number: 2022901199

First edition

10 9 8 7 6 5 4 3 2 1

Design by Mary Zadroga
The text is set in Albus Regular and Museo Slab 700.
The titles are set in Pocket Bold.
The illustrations are done digitally in Photoshop.

CONTENTs

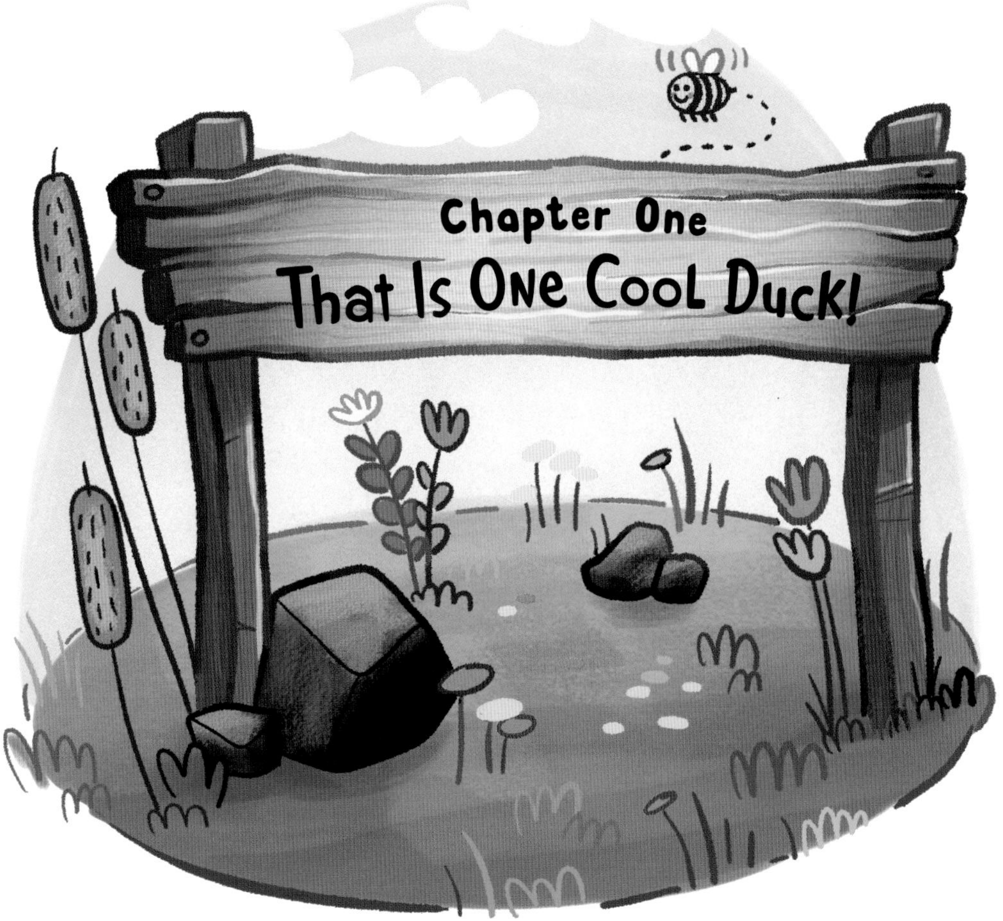
Chapter One
That Is One Cool Duck!

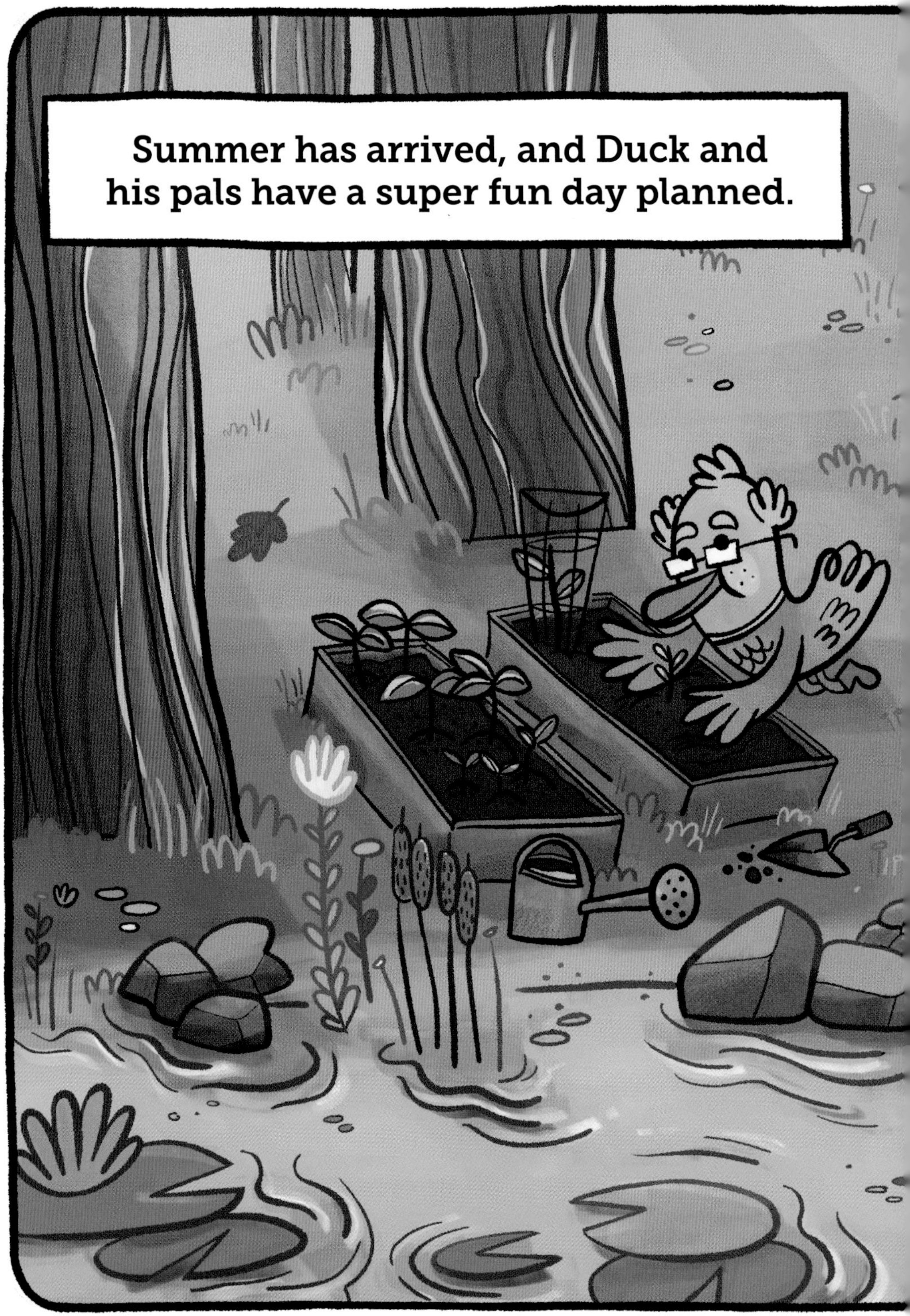
Summer has arrived, and Duck and his pals have a super fun day planned.

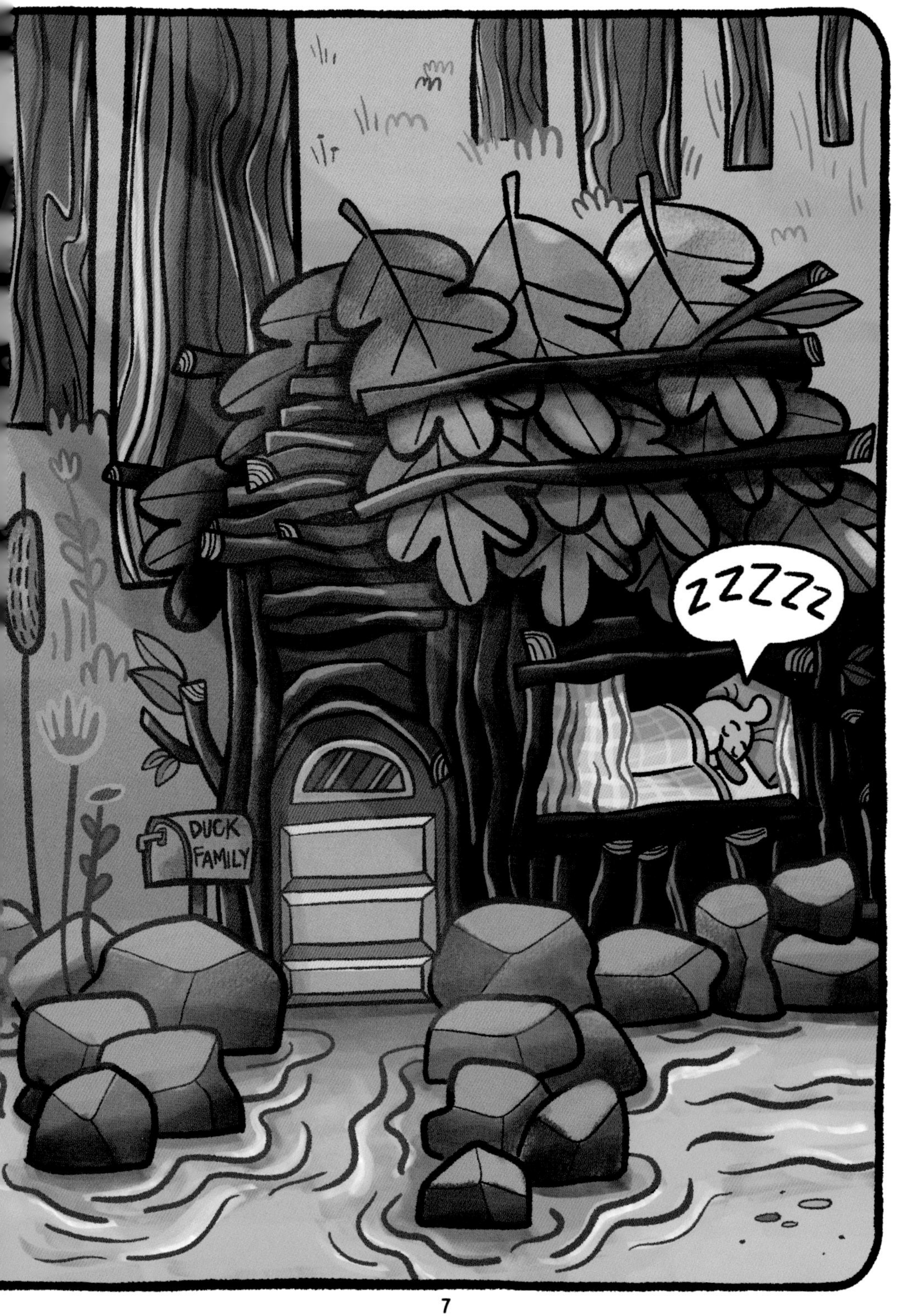
DUCK FAMILY
ZZZZZ

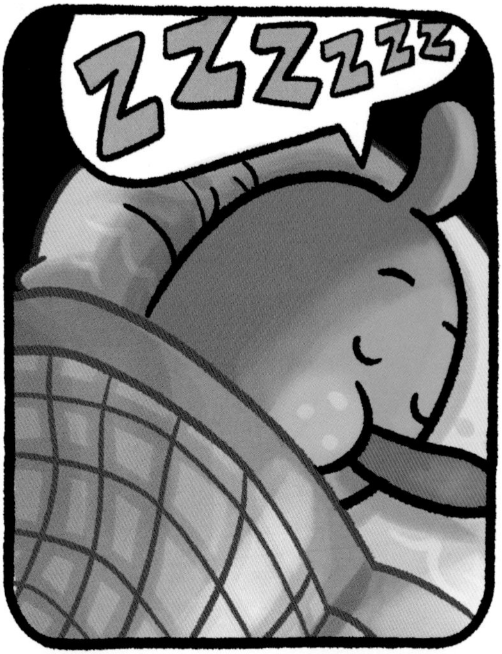
ZZZzzz

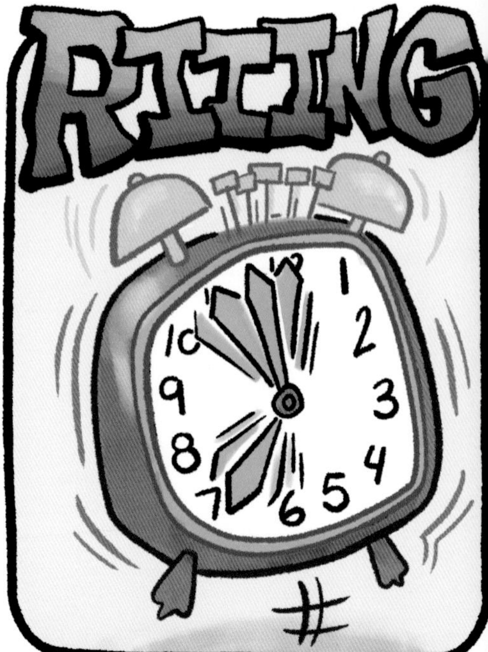
RIIING

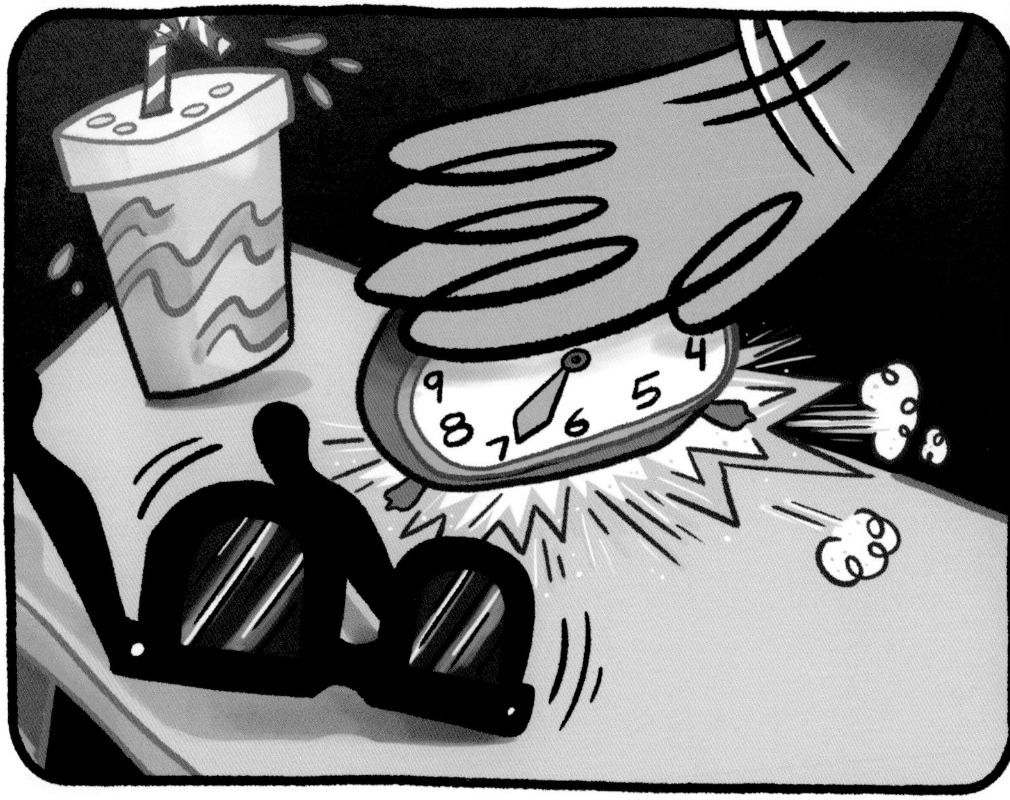

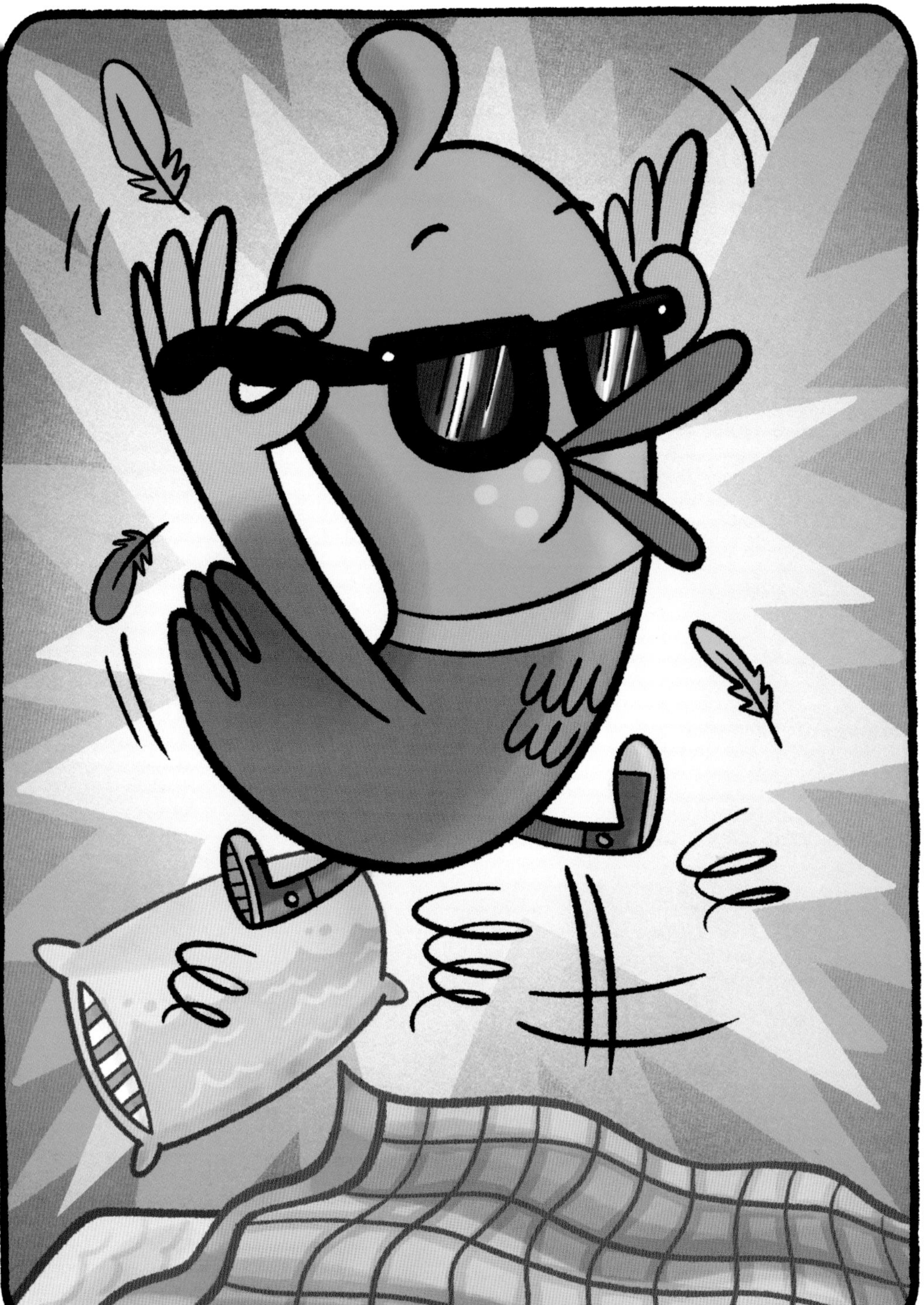

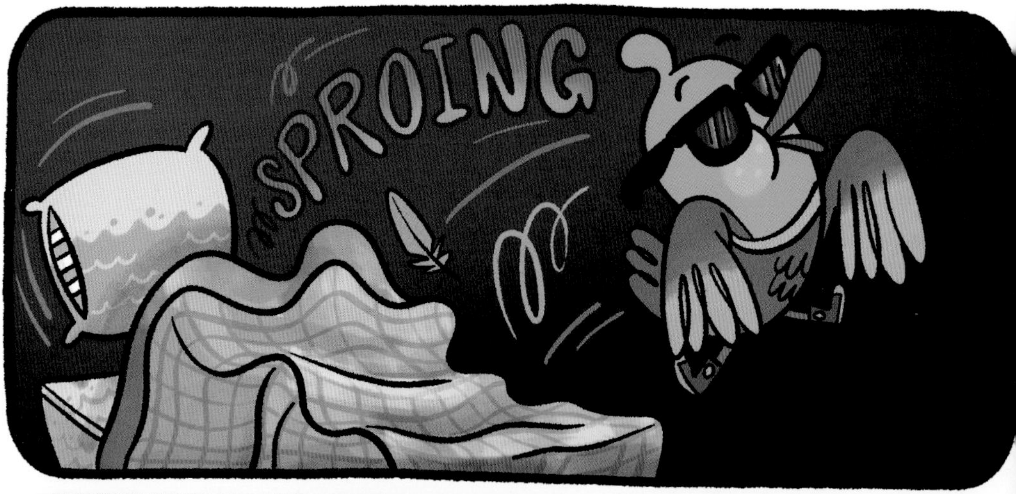
SPROING

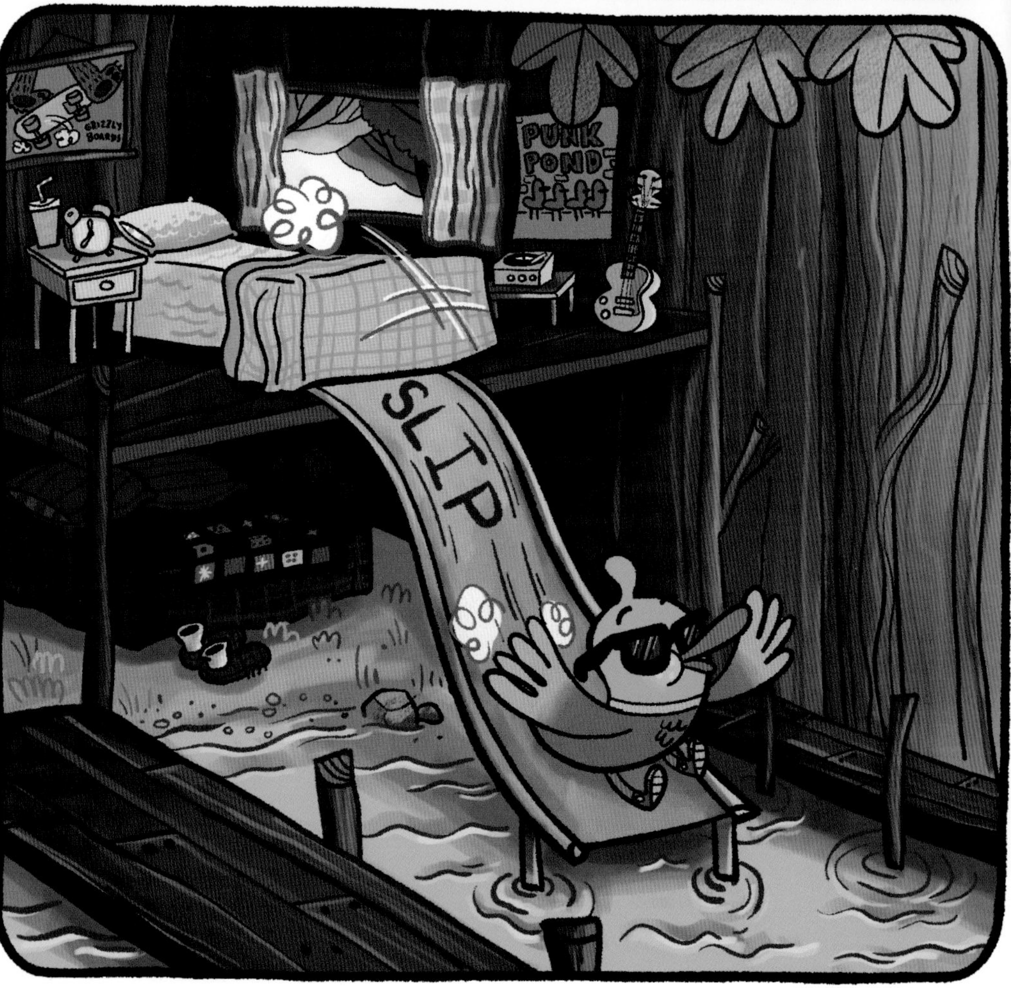
GRIZZLY BOARDS
PUNK POND
SLIP

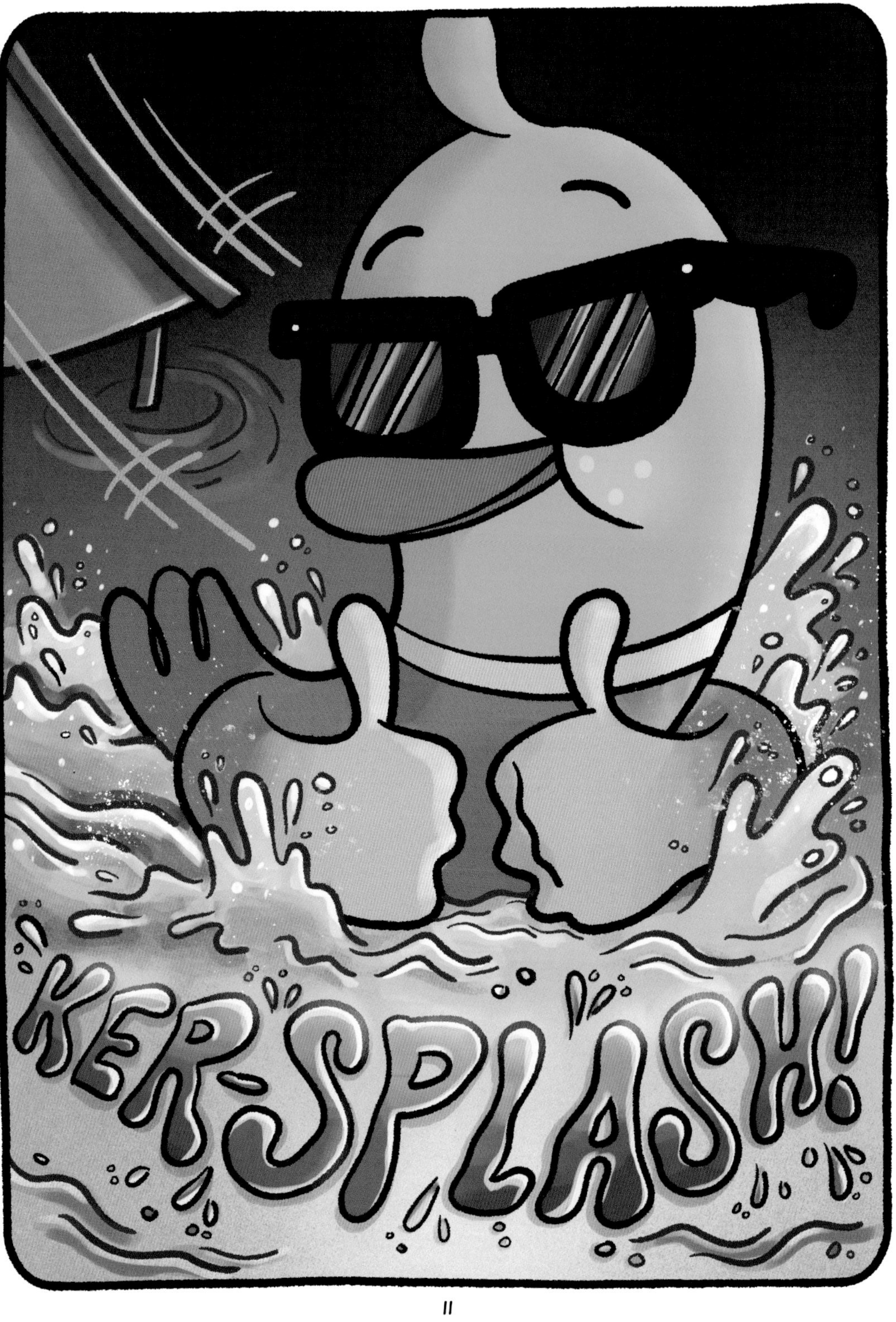
KER-SPLASH!

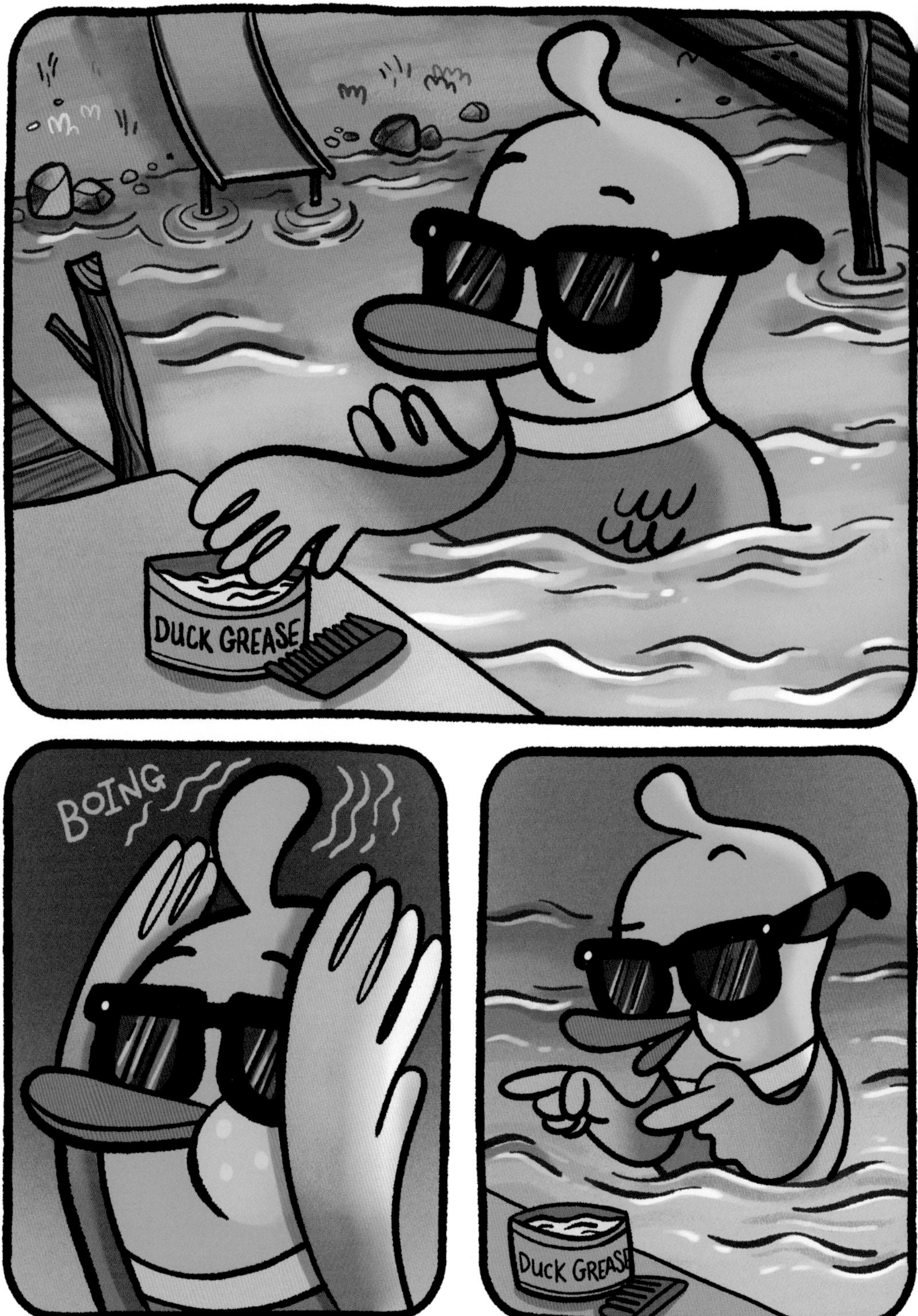
DUCK GREASE
BOING
DUCK GREASE

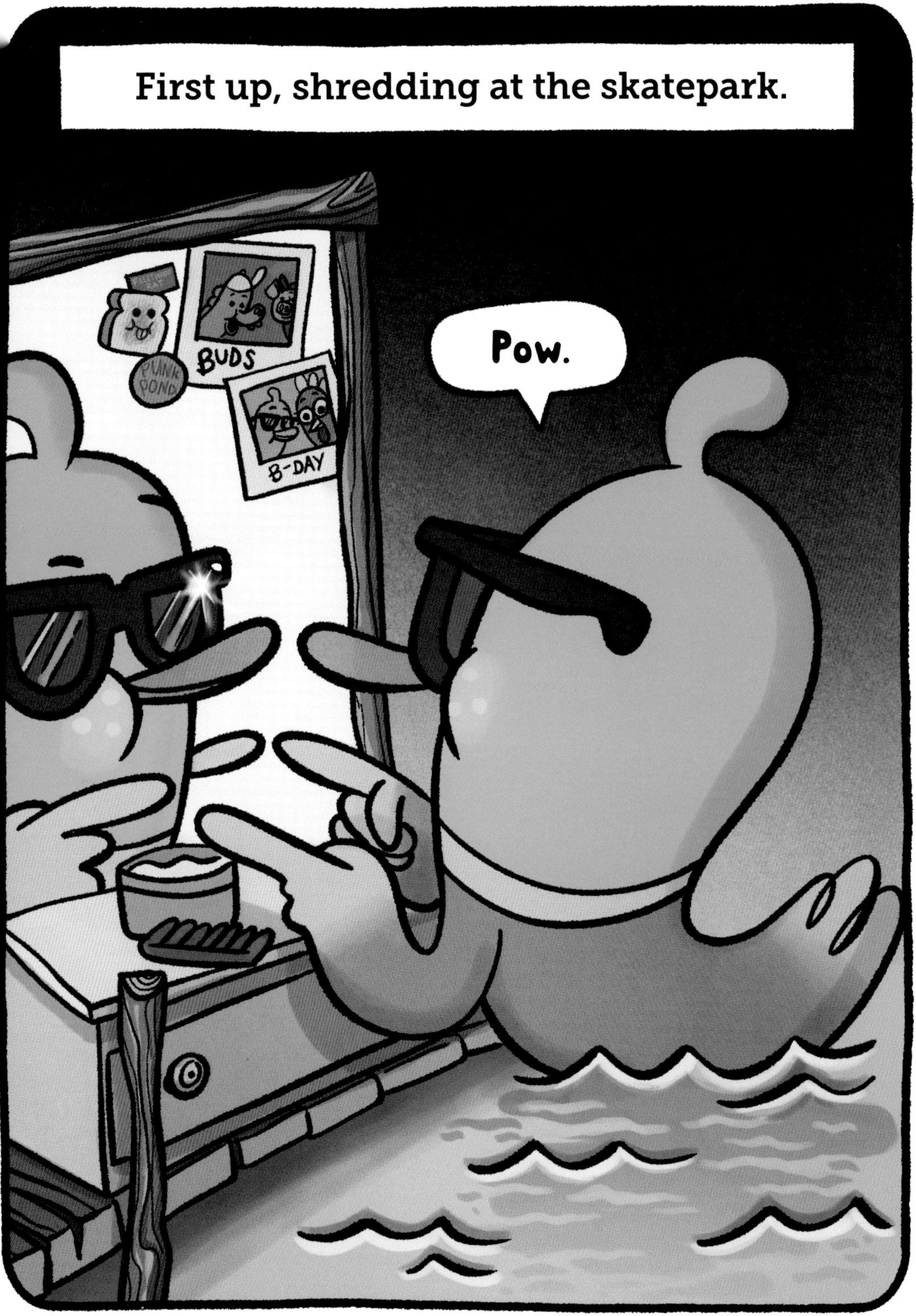
First up, shredding at the skatepark.
Pow.
BUDS
PUNK POND
B-DAY

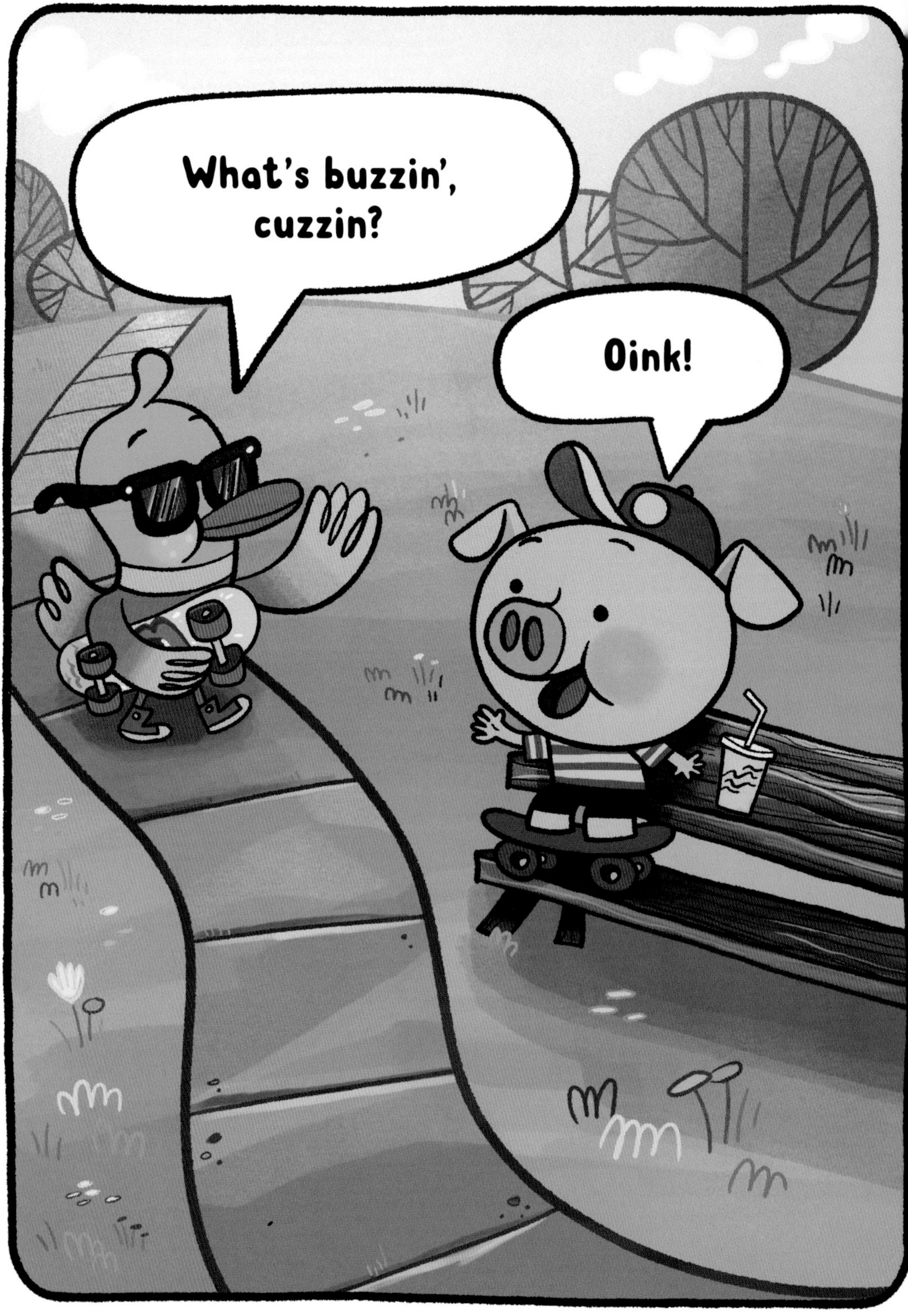
What's buzzin',
cuzzin?
Oink!

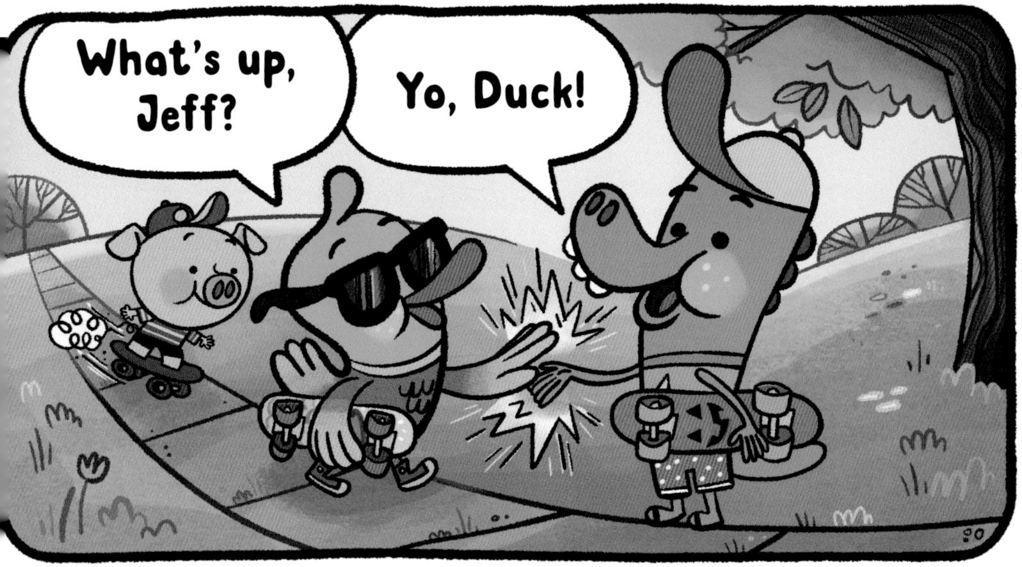
What's up, Jeff?
Yo, Duck!

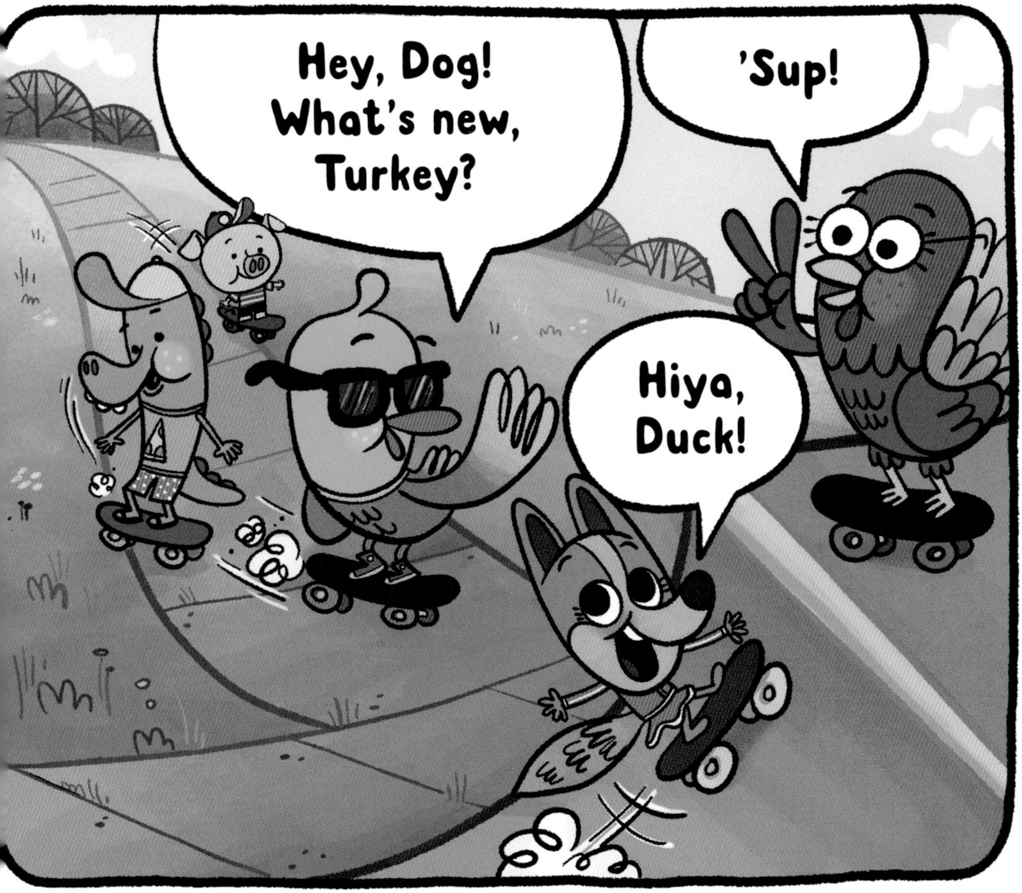
Hey, Dog! What's new, Turkey?
'Sup!
Hiya, Duck!

Duck can kickflip on a skateboard.

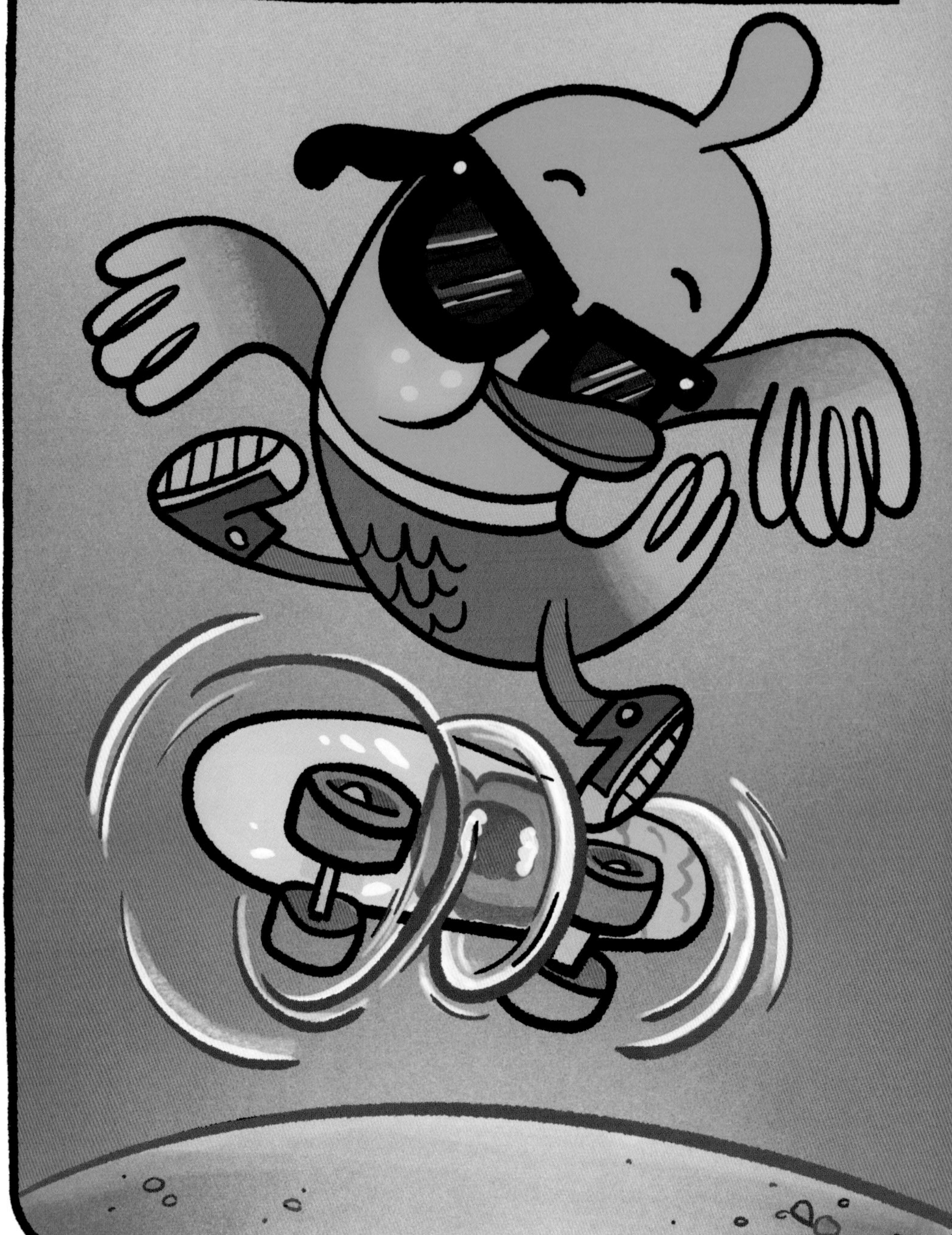

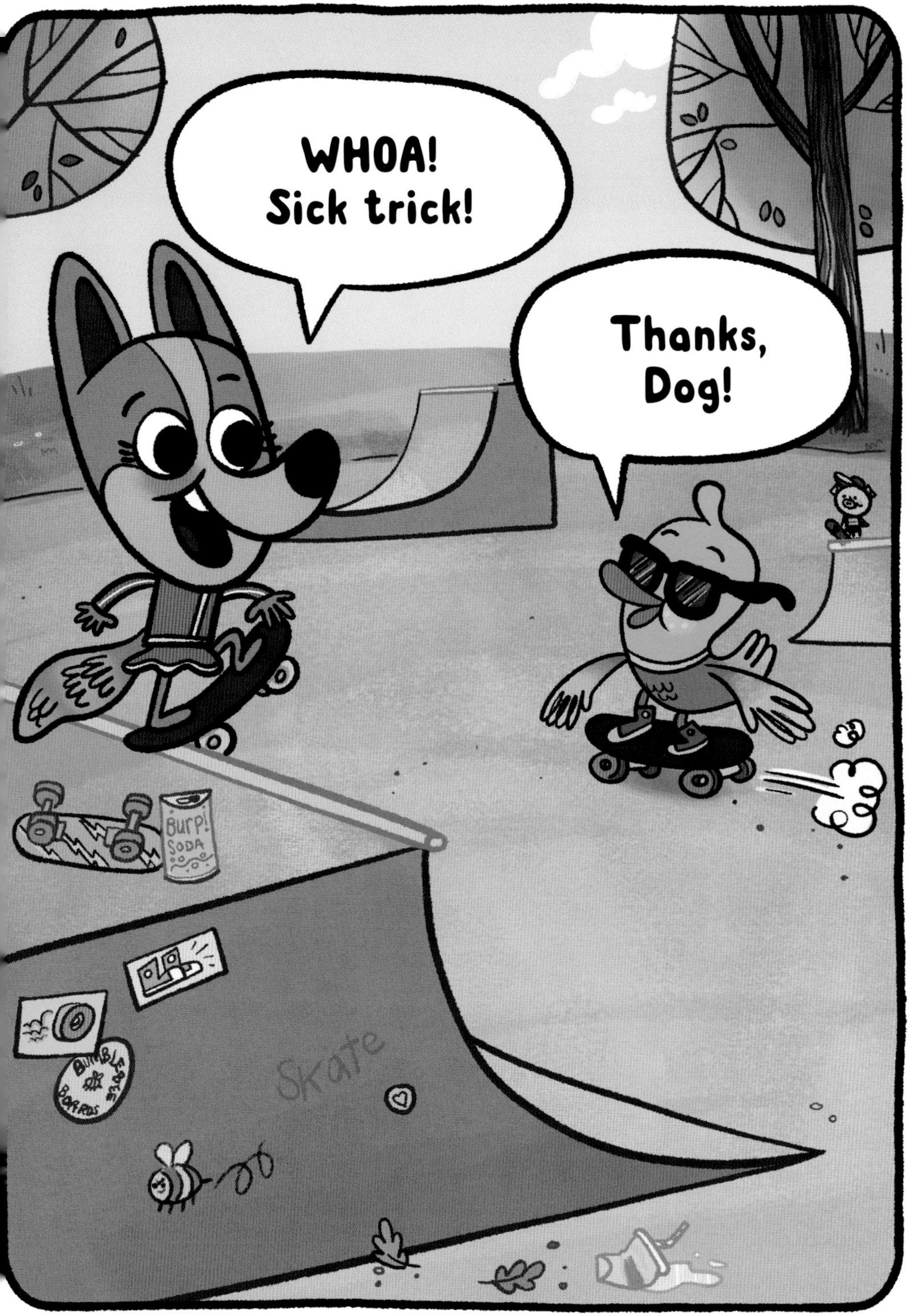
WHOA!
Sick trick!
Thanks,
Dog!
BURP! SODA
BUMBLE BOARDS
Skate

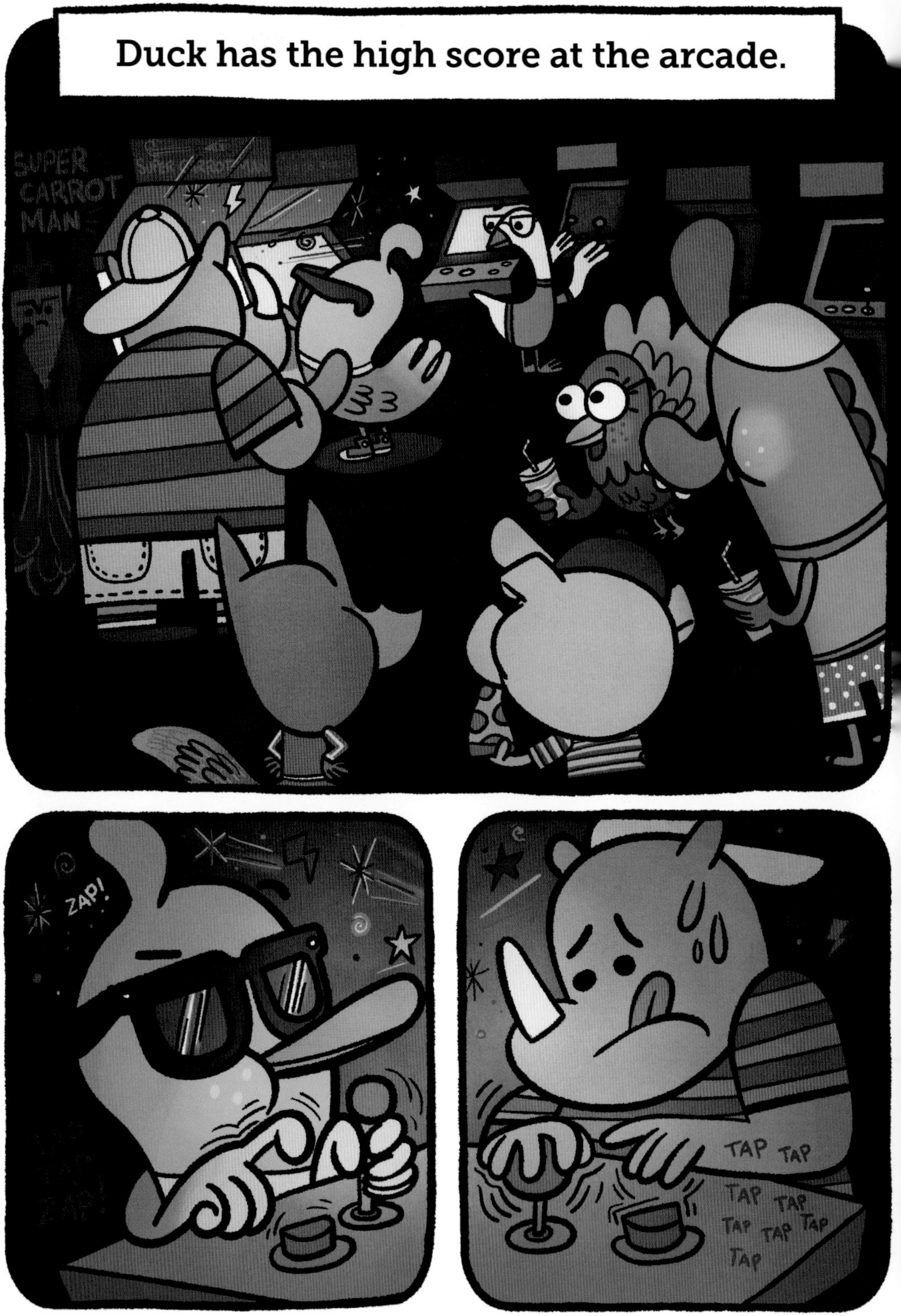
Duck has the high score at the arcade.
SUPER CARROT MAN
ZAP!
TAP TAP
TAP TAP
TAP TAP TAP
TAP

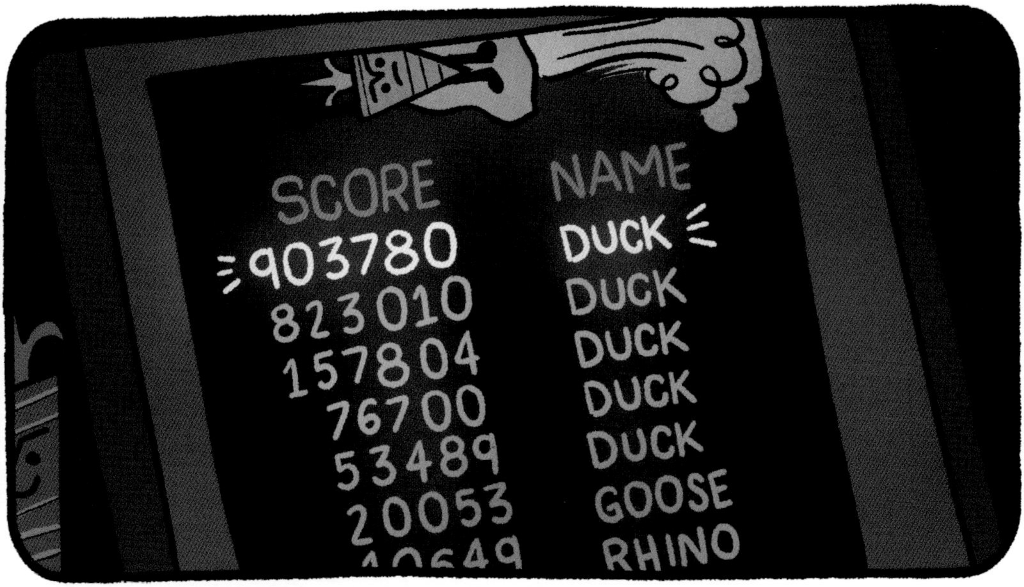
SCORE
NAME
903780
DUCK
823010
DUCK
157804
DUCK
76700
DUCK
53489
DUCK
20053
GOOSE
RHINO

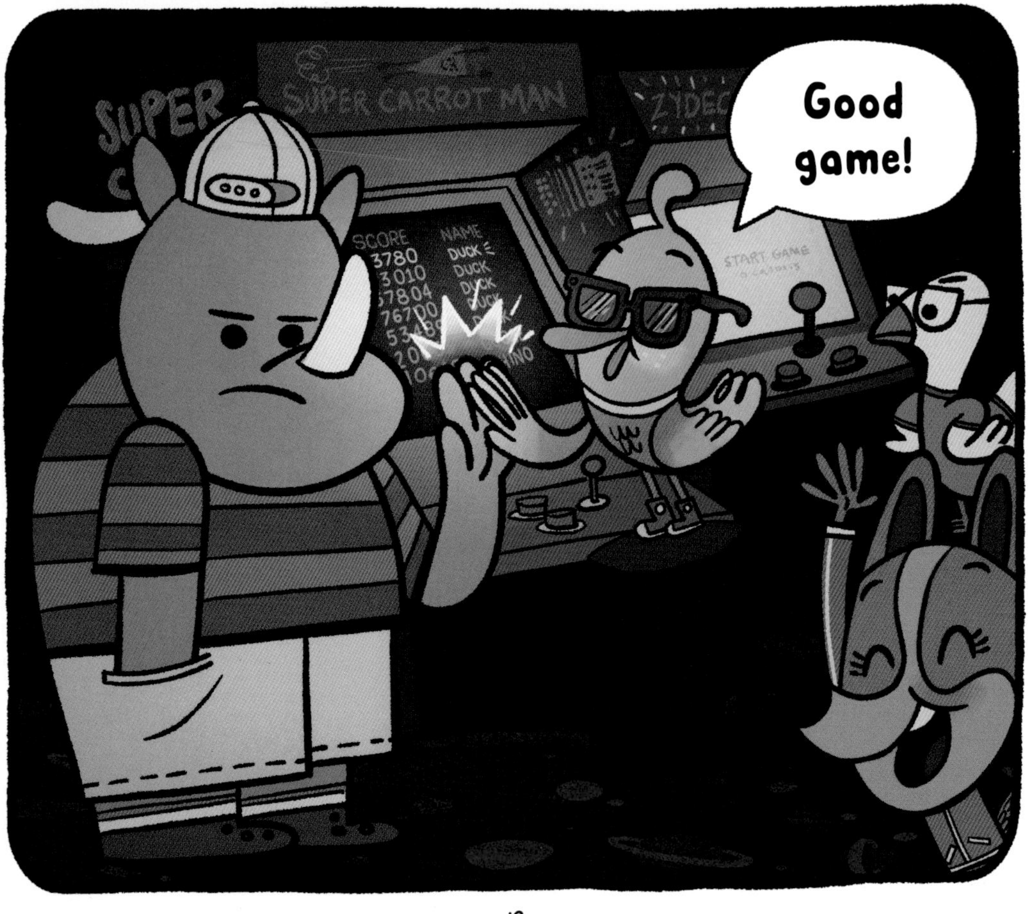
SUPER
SUPER CARROT MAN
START GAME
Good game!

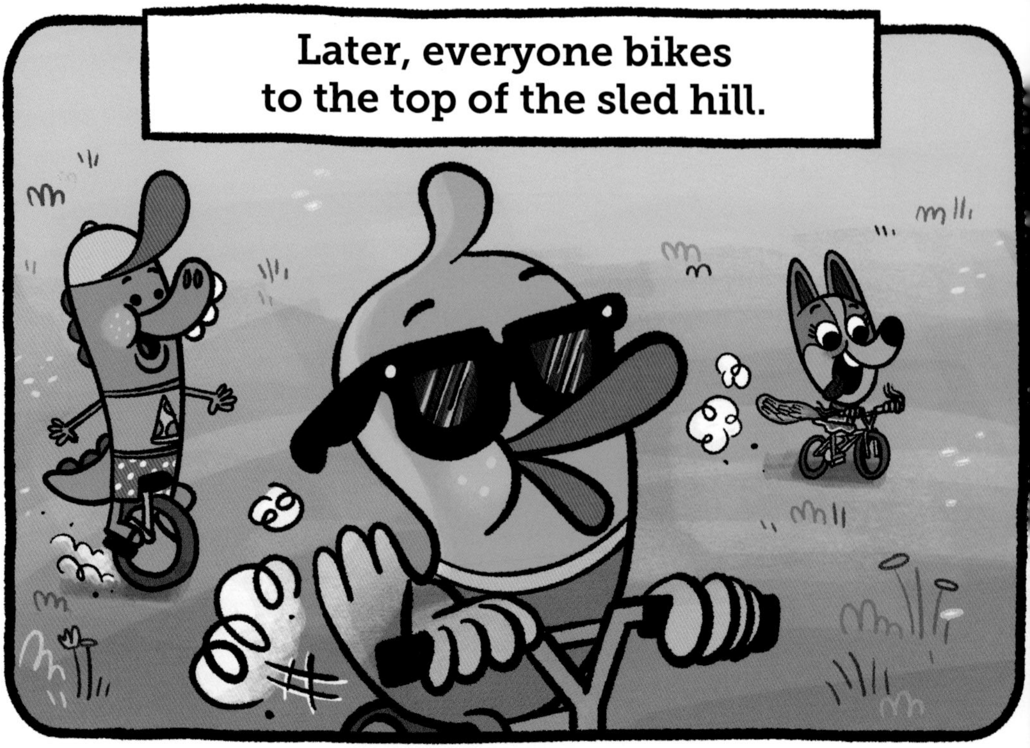
Later, everyone bikes to the top of the sled hill.

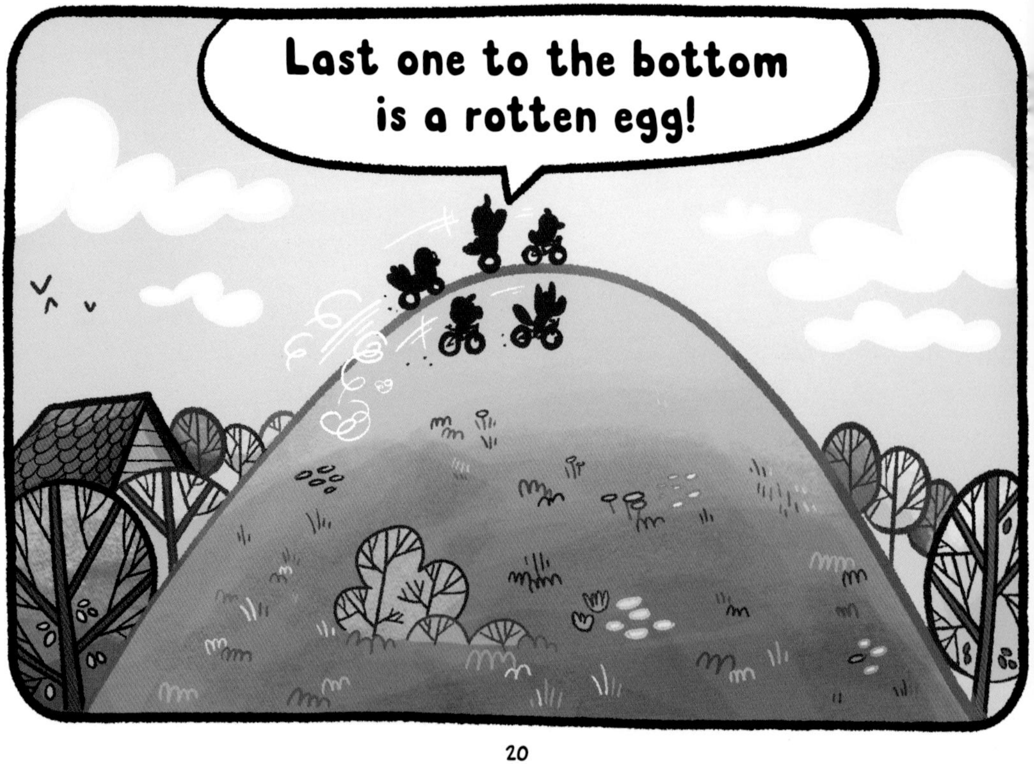
Last one to the bottom is a rotten egg!

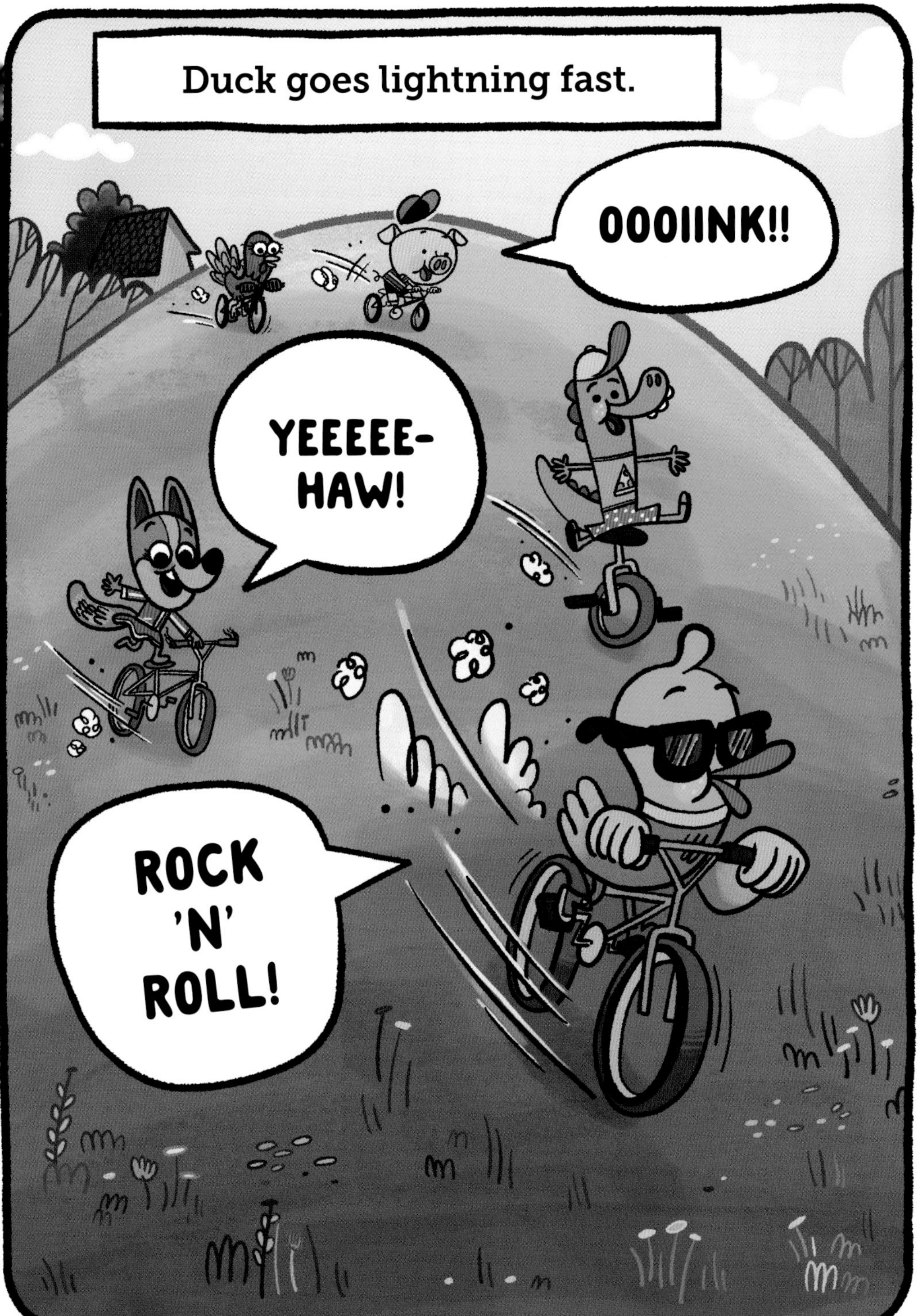
Duck goes lightning fast.
OOOIINK!!
YEEEEE-HAW!
ROCK 'N' ROLL!

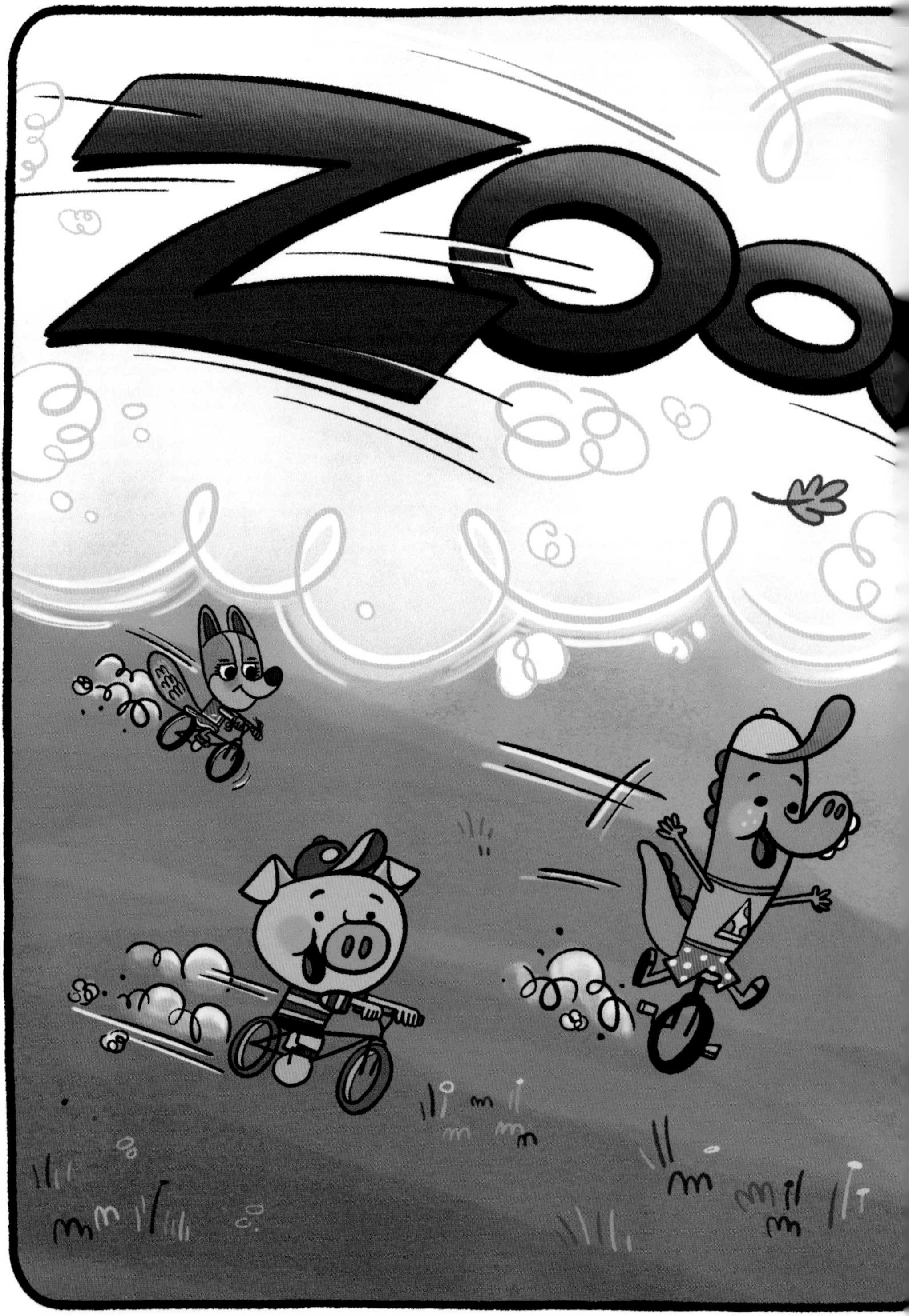
ZOO

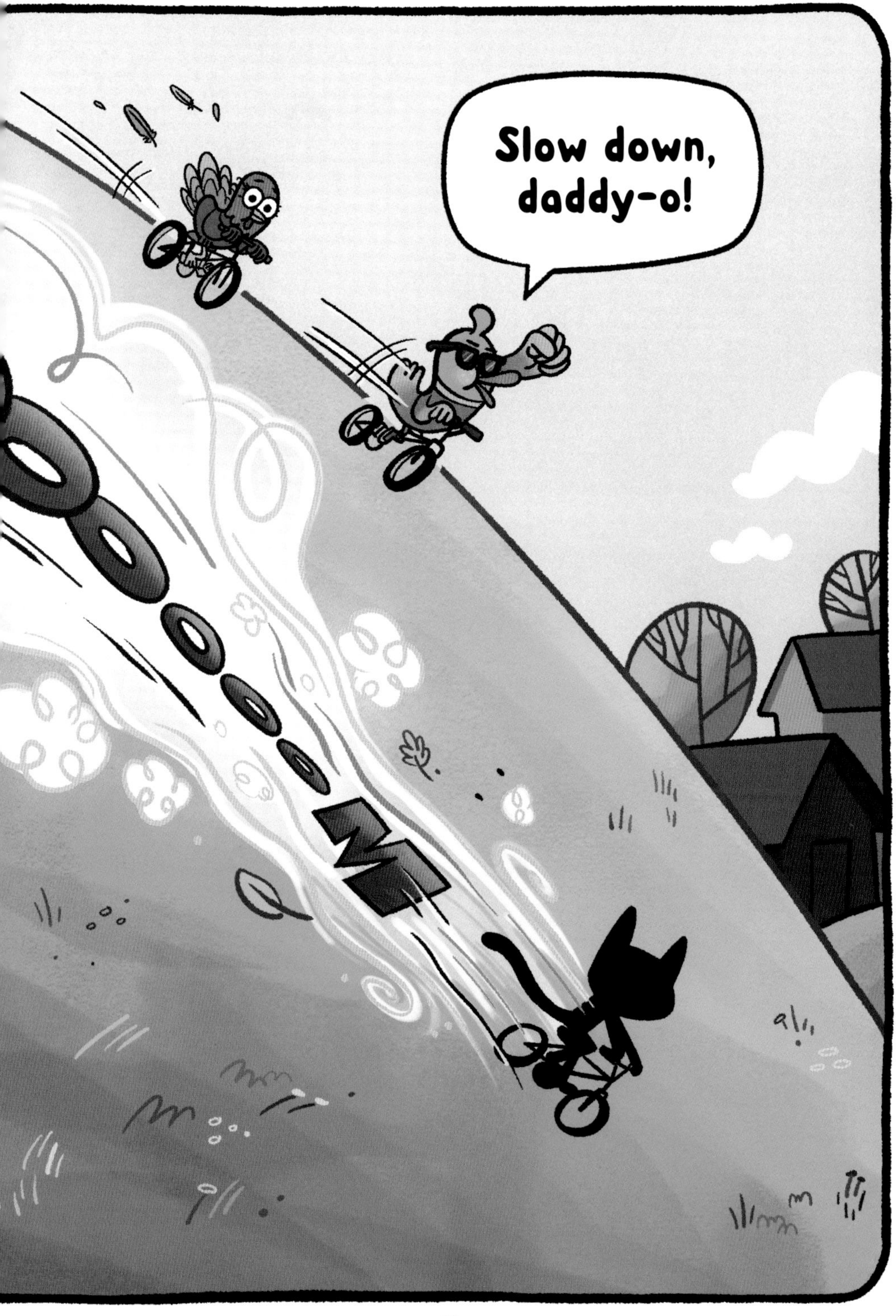
Slow down, daddy-o!

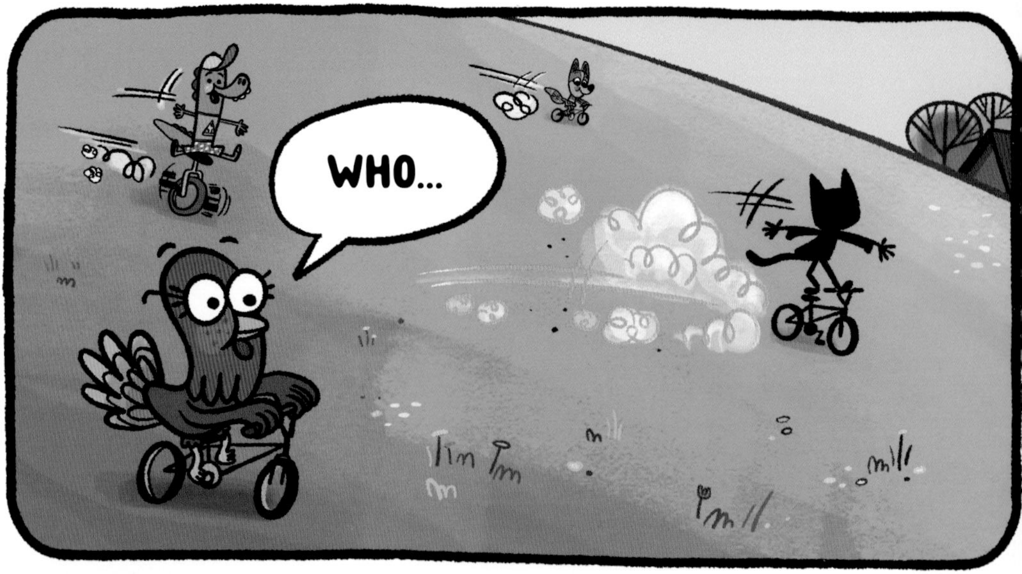
WHO...

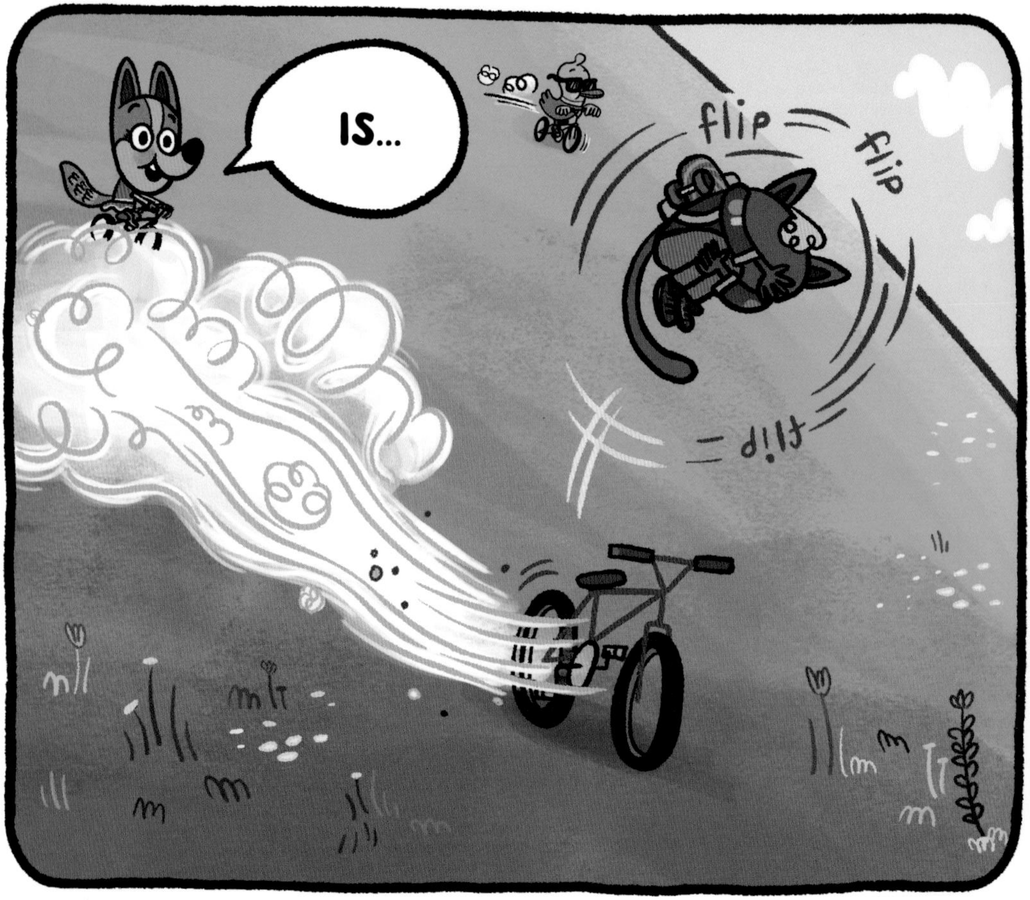
IS...
flip
flip
flip

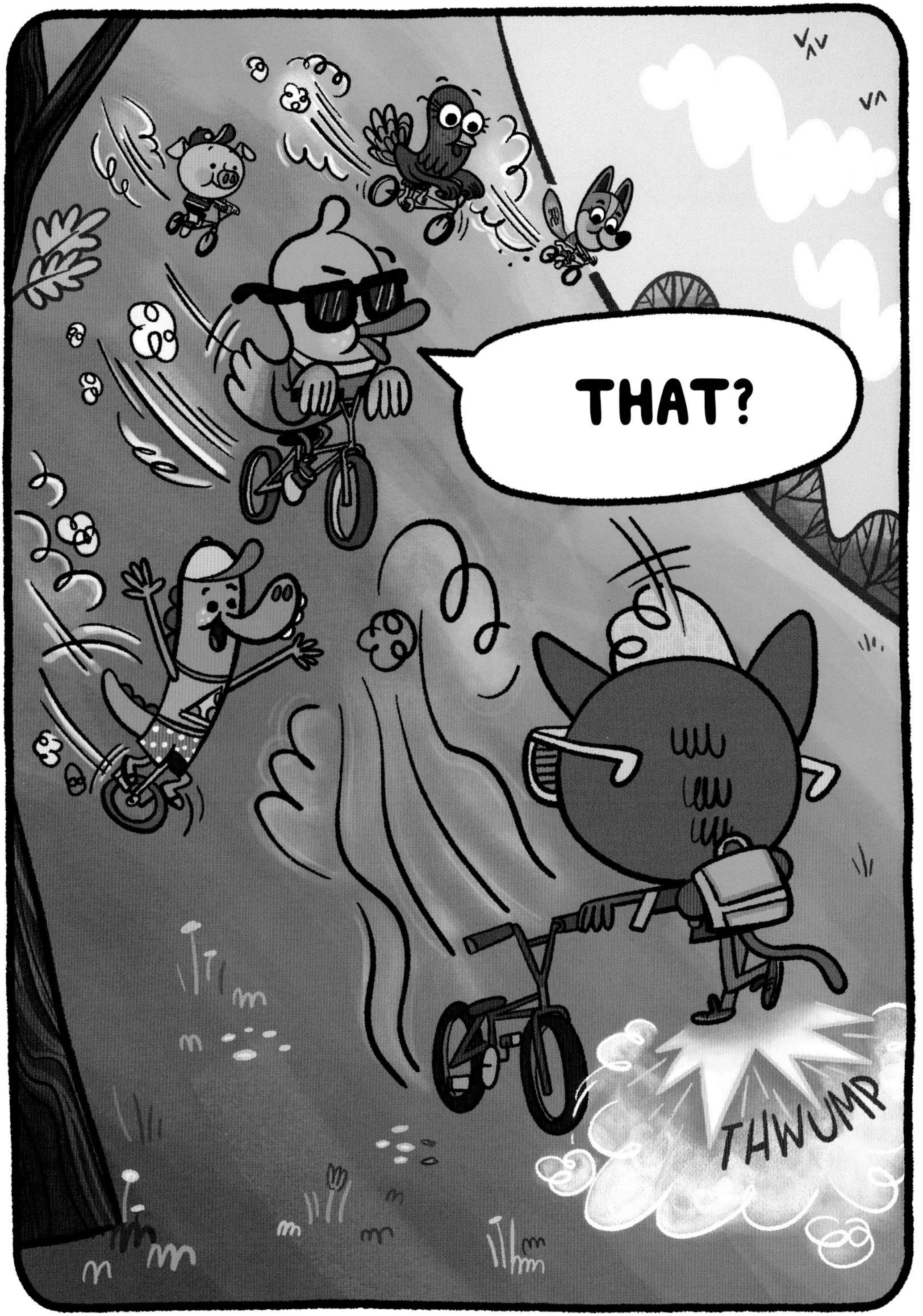
THAT?
THWUMP

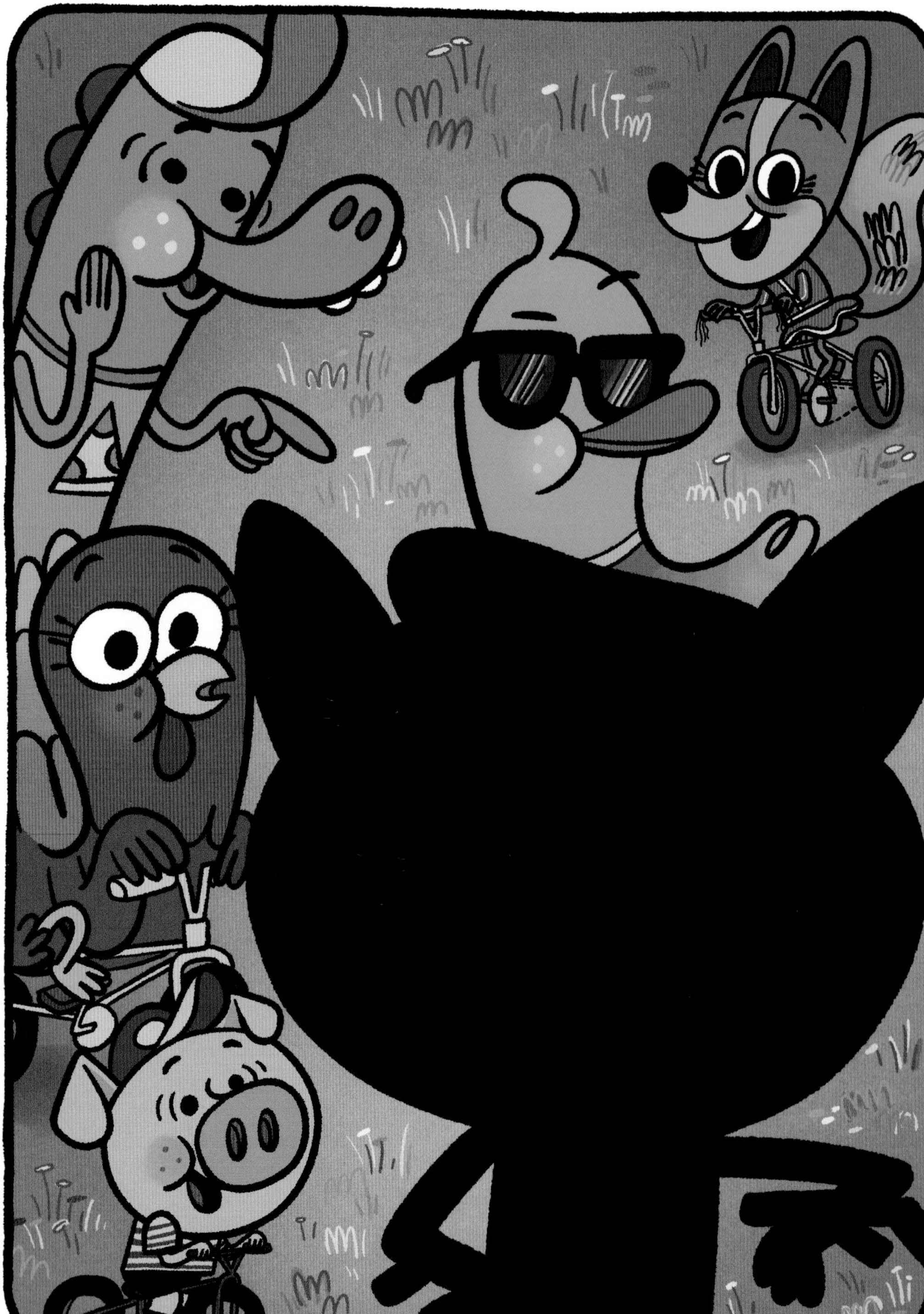

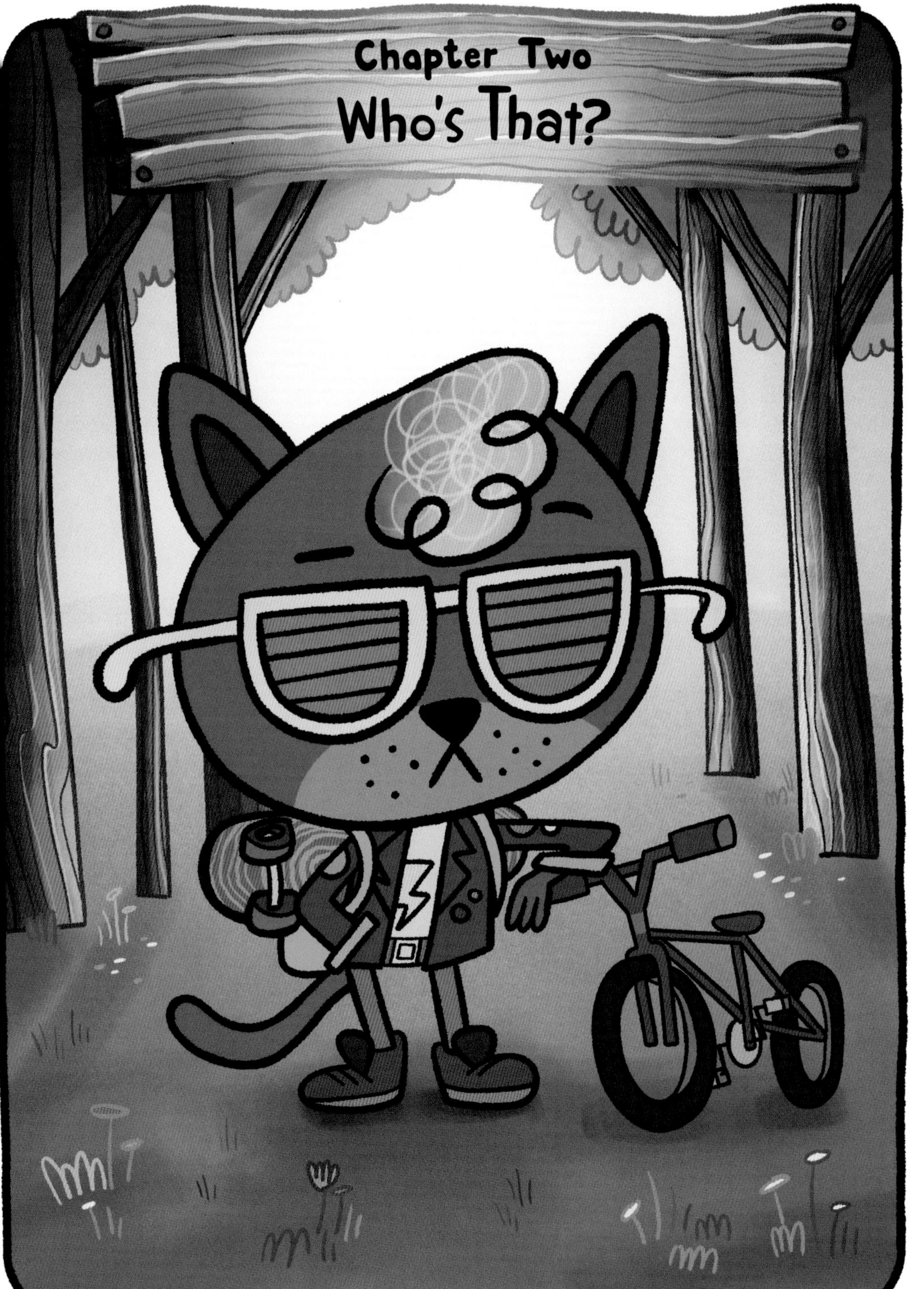
Chapter Two
Who's That?

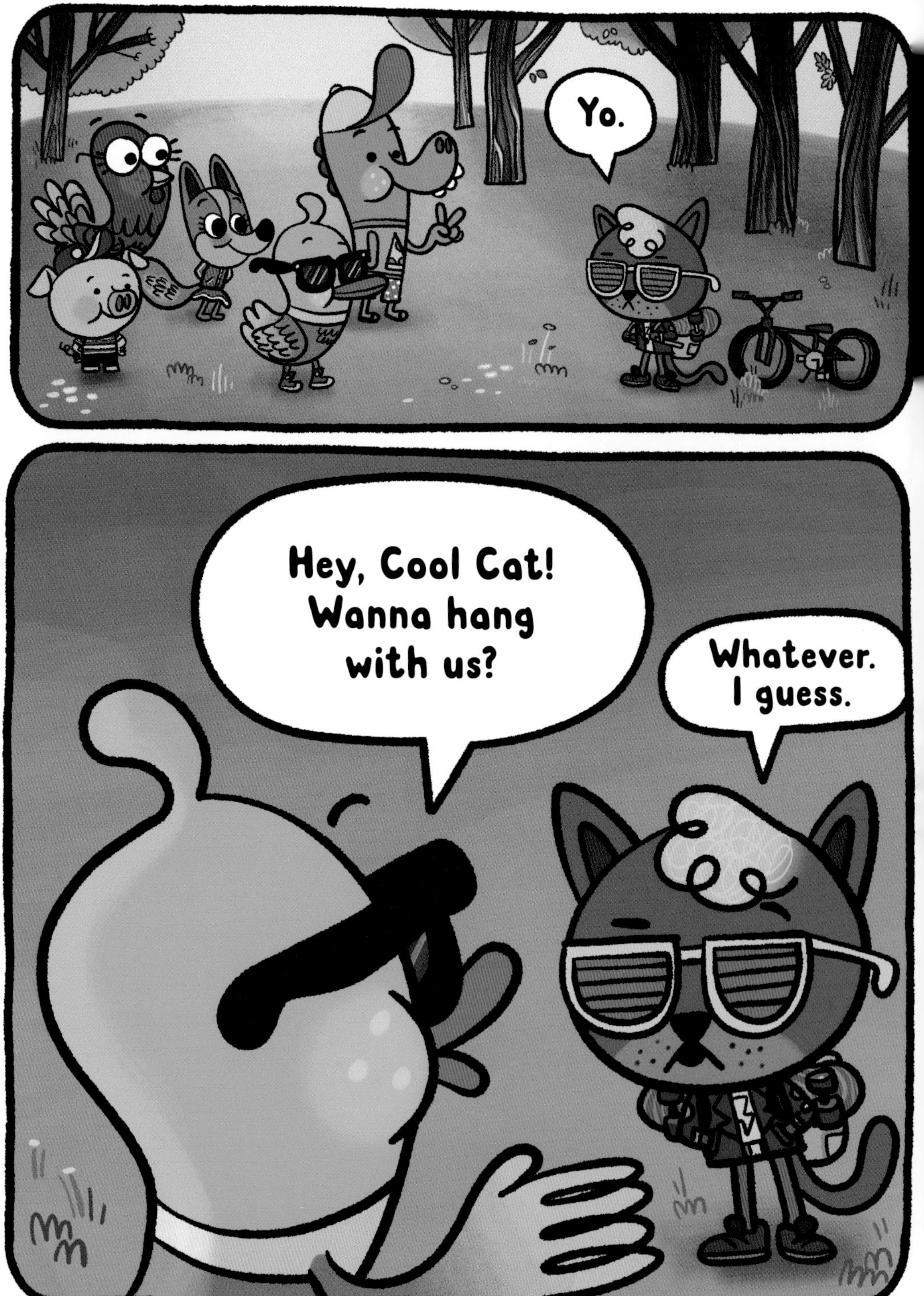
Yo.
Hey, Cool Cat! Wanna hang with us?
Whatever. I guess.

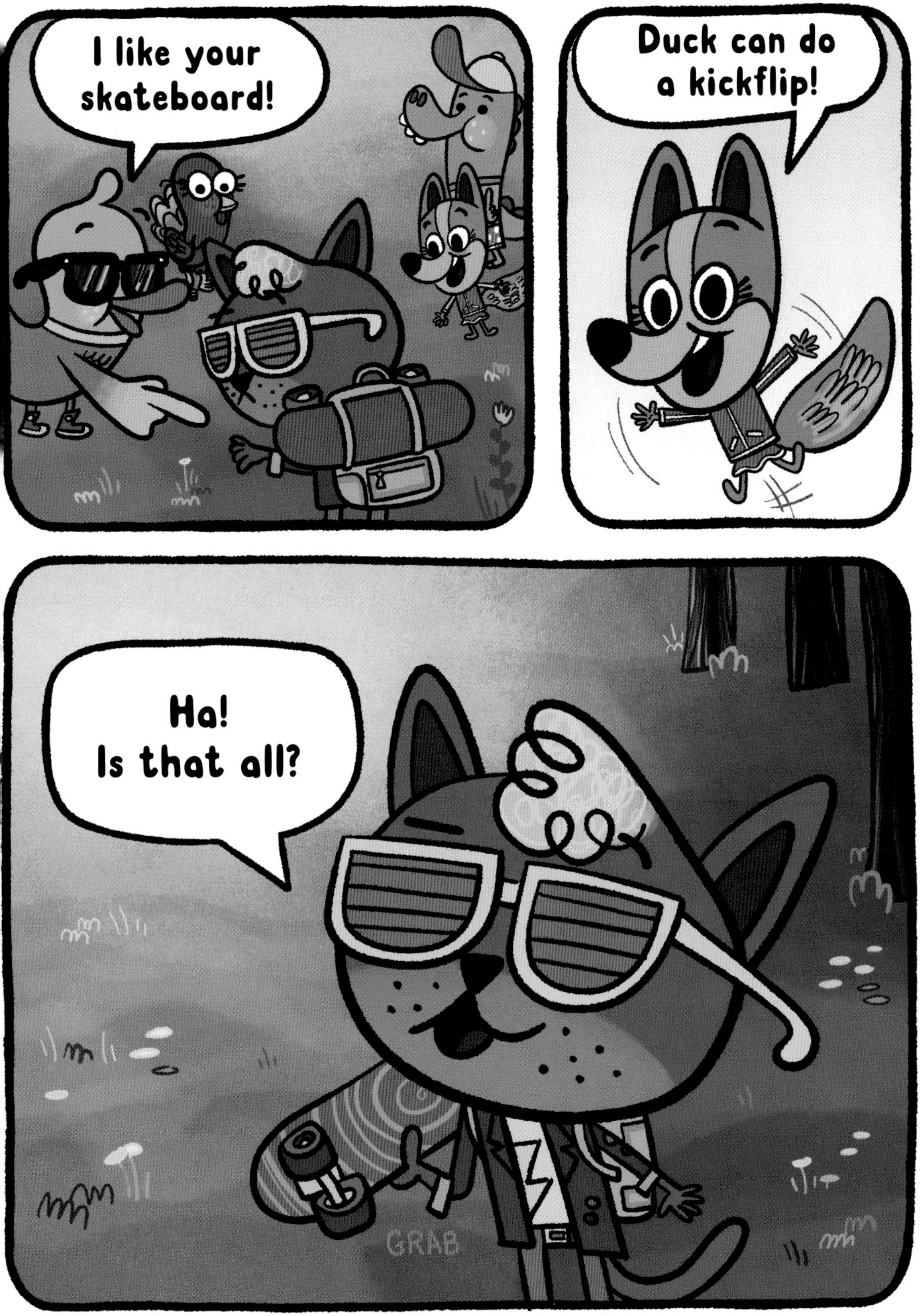
I like your skateboard!
Duck can do a kickflip!
Ha! Is that all?
GRAB

Cat surprises everyone with a triple kickflip.

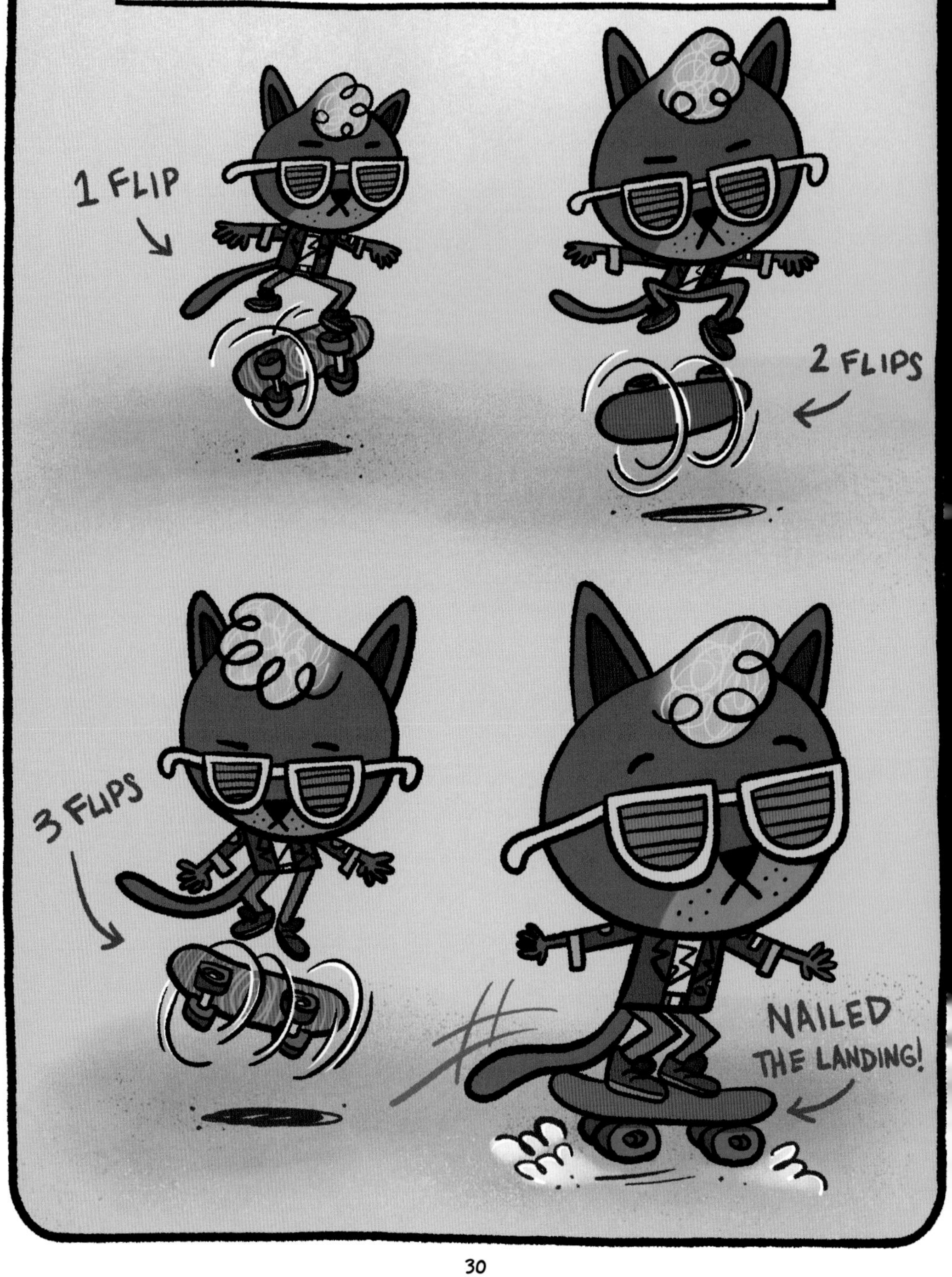
1 FLIP
2 FLIPS
3 FLIPS
NAILED THE LANDING!

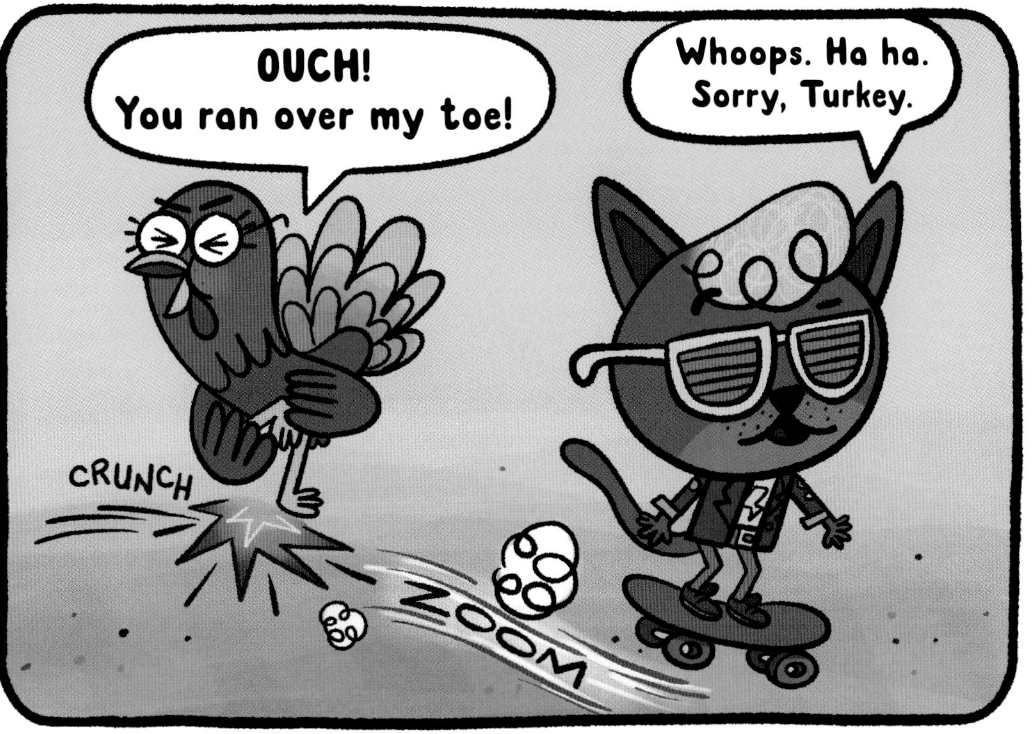
OUCH!
You ran over my toe!
Whoops. Ha ha.
Sorry, Turkey.
CRUNCH
ZOOM

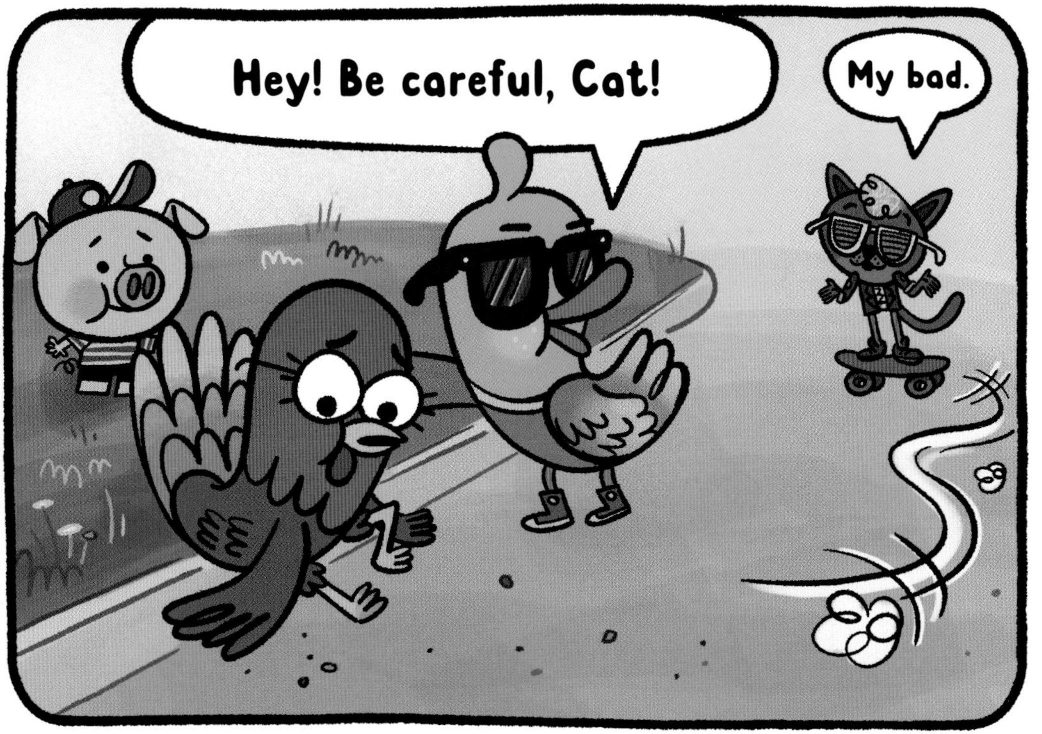
Hey! Be careful, Cat!
My bad.

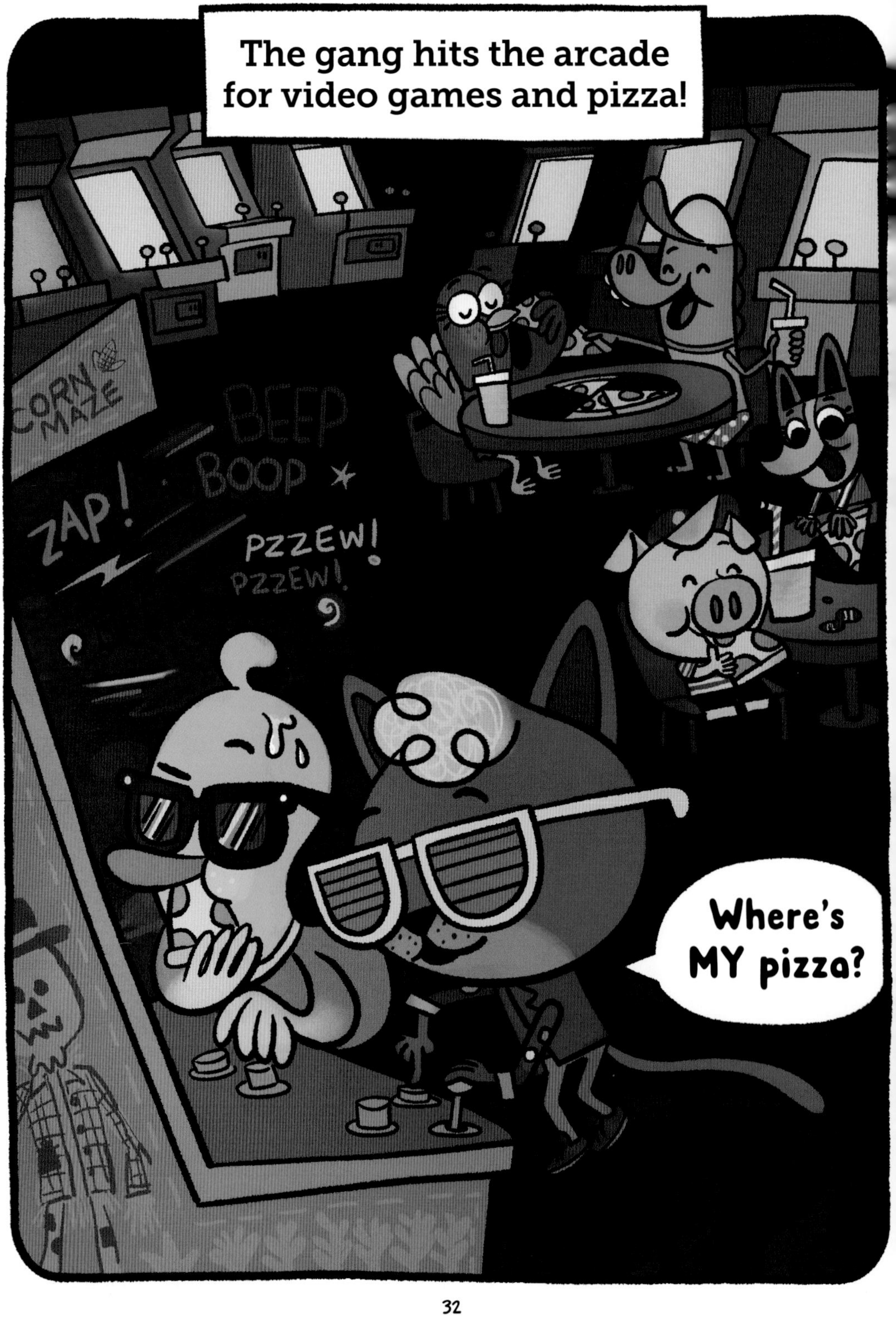
The gang hits the arcade for video games and pizza!
CORN MAZE
BEEP
BOOP
ZAP!
PZZEW!
PZZEW!
Where's MY pizza?

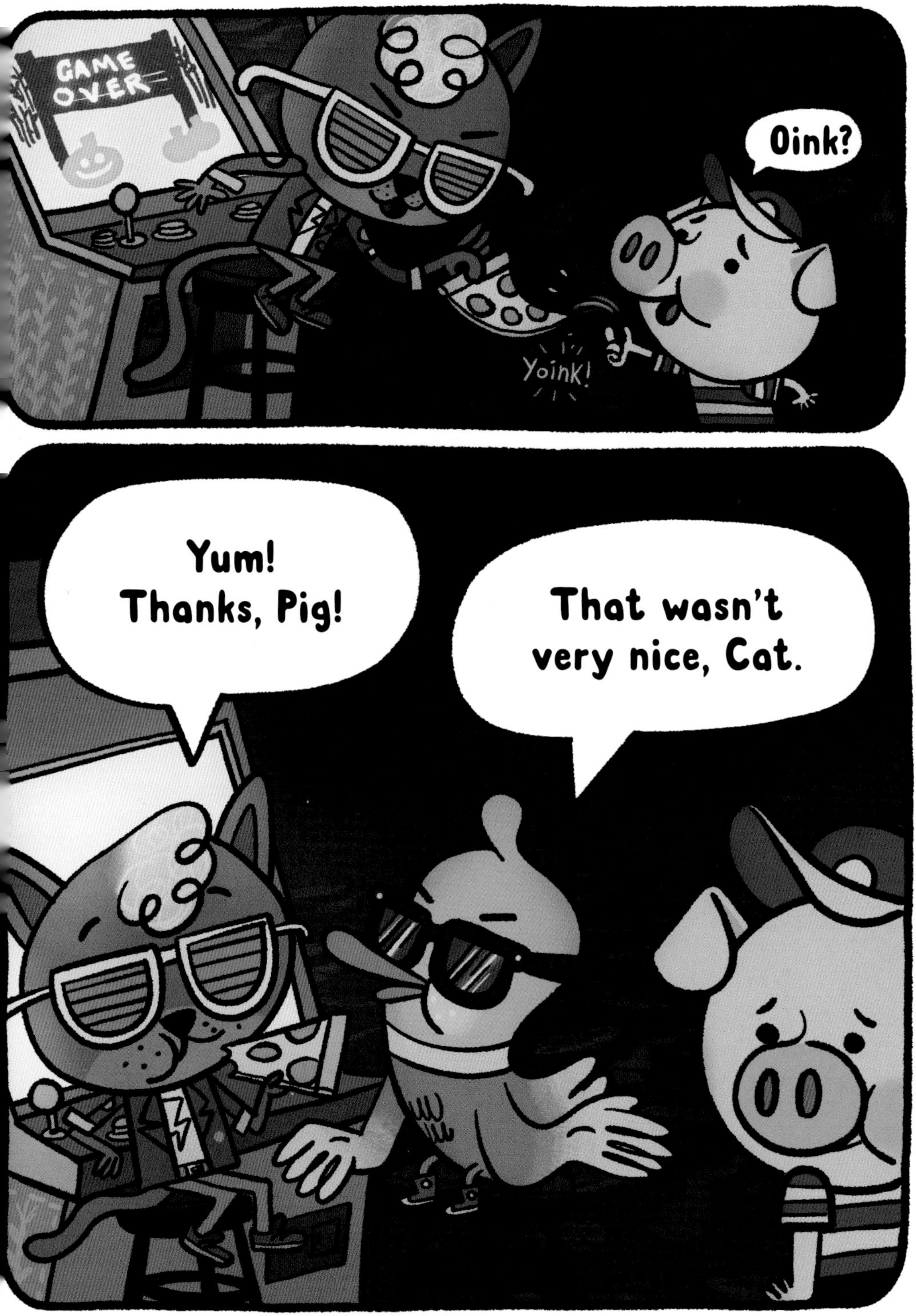
GAME OVER
Oink?
Yoink!
Yum! Thanks, Pig!
That wasn't very nice, Cat.

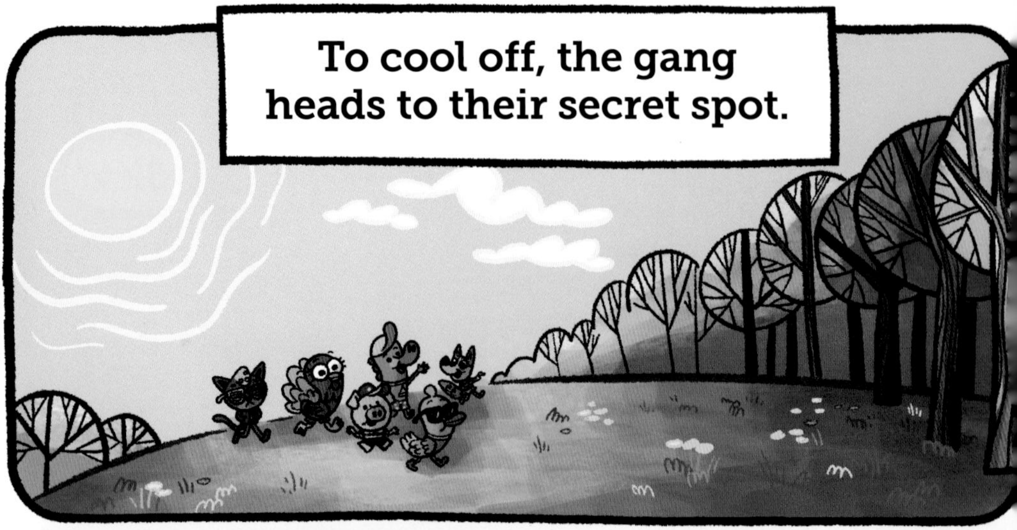
To cool off, the gang heads to their secret spot.

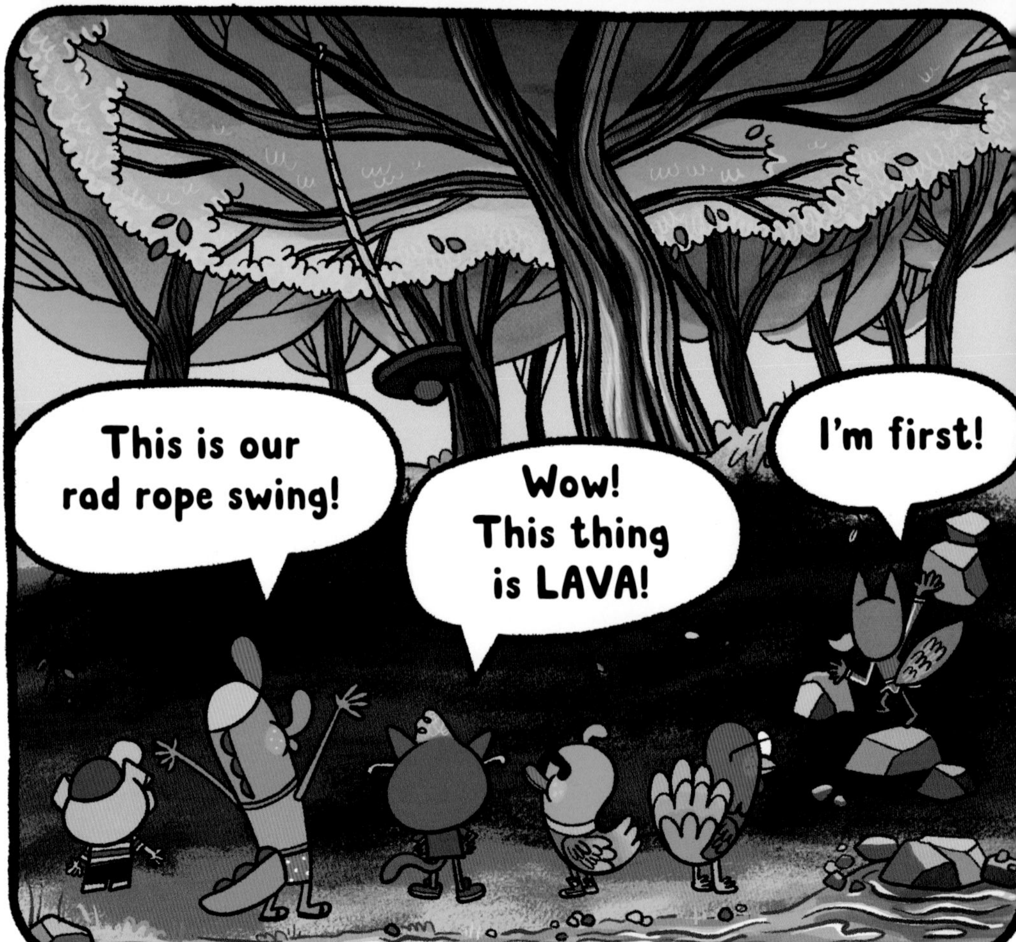
This is our rad rope swing!
Wow! This thing is LAVA!
I'm first!

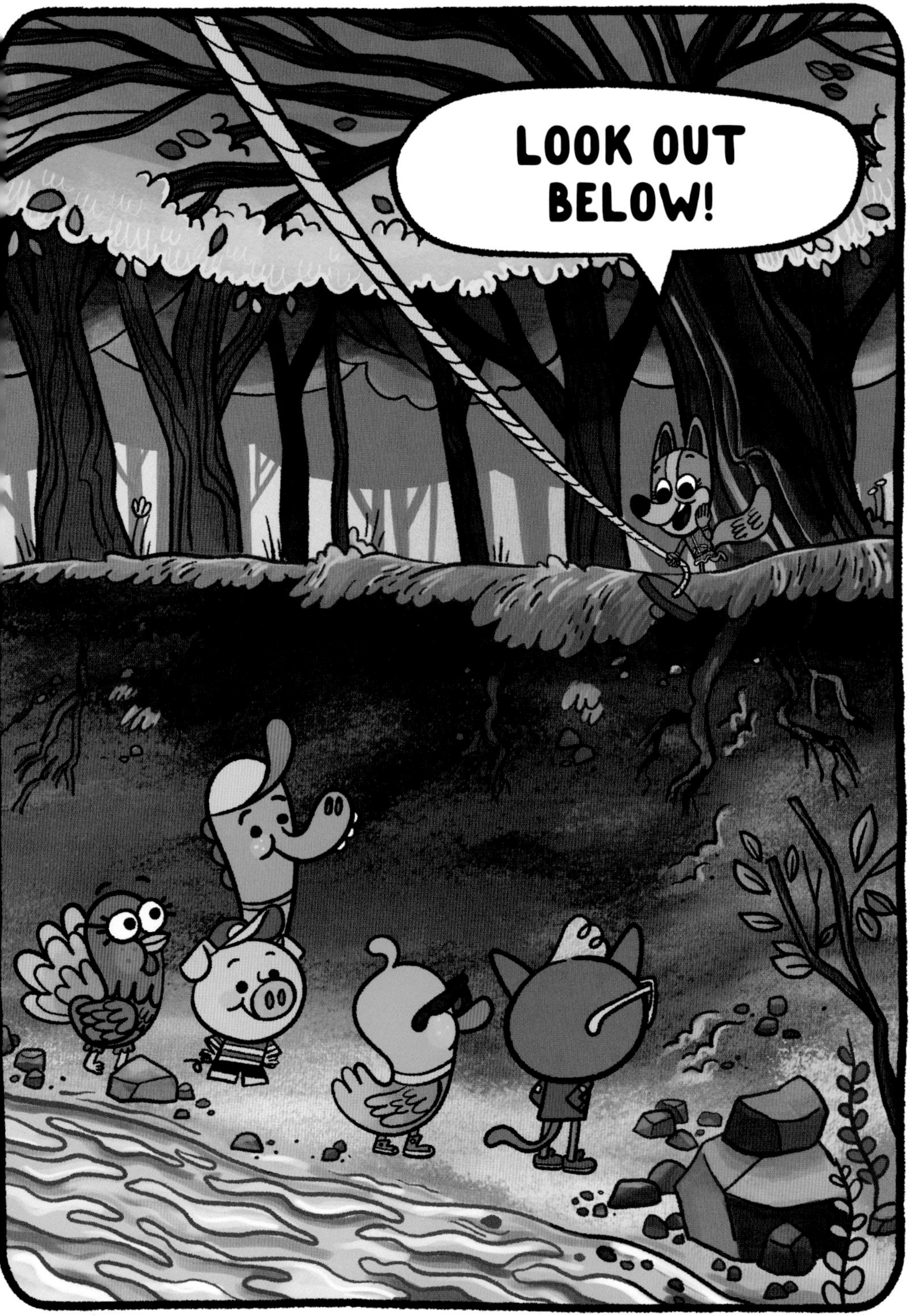
LOOK OUT BELOW!

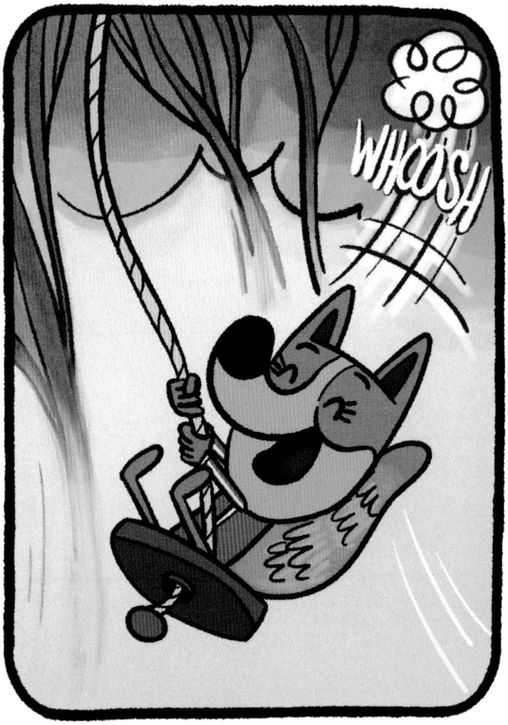
WHOOSH

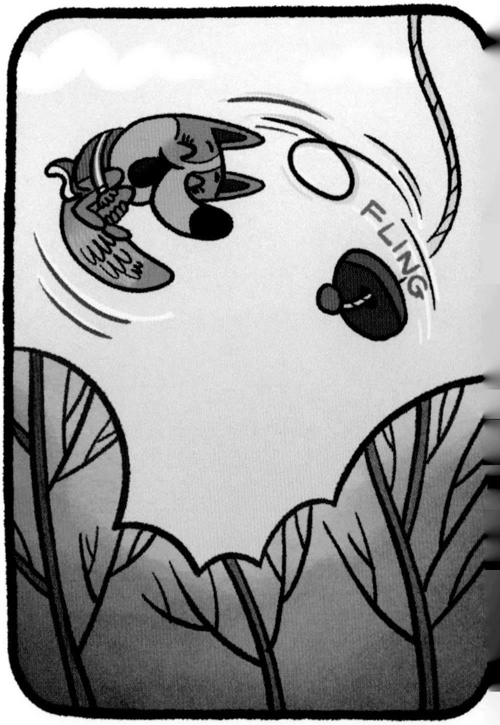
FLING

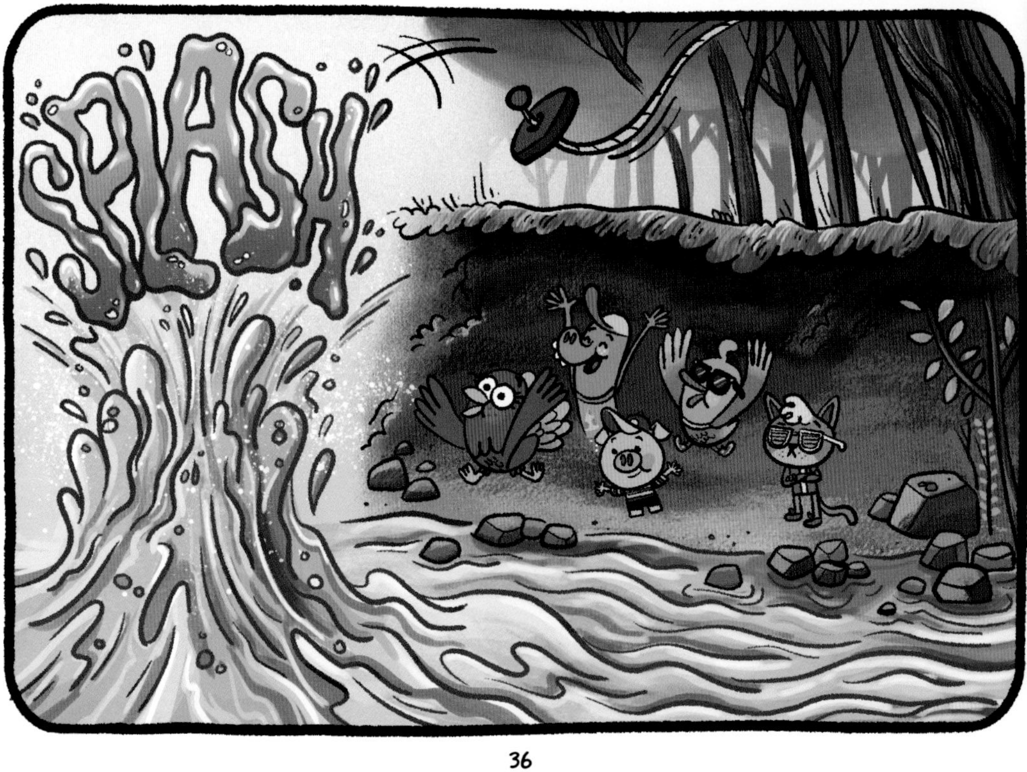
SPLASH

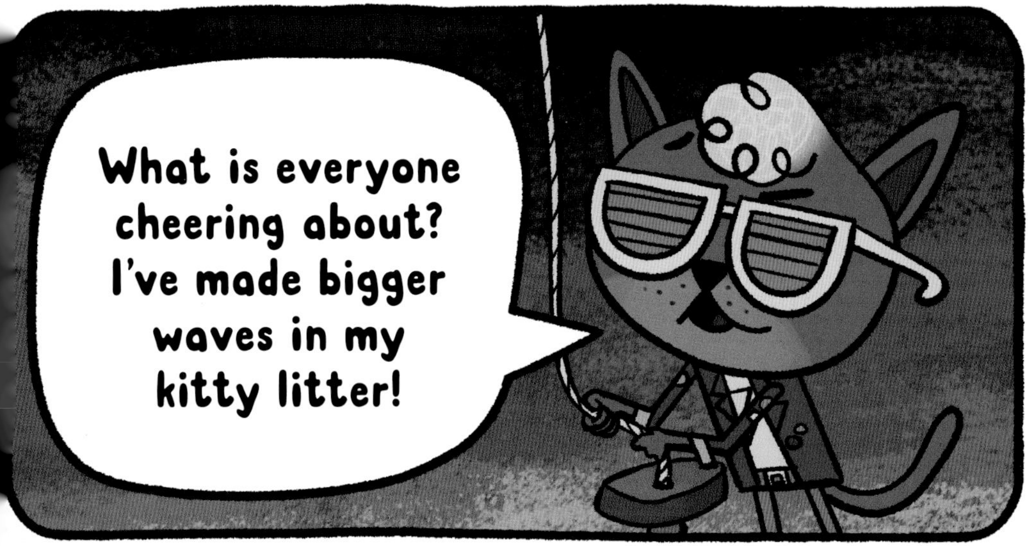
What is everyone cheering about? I've made bigger waves in my kitty litter!

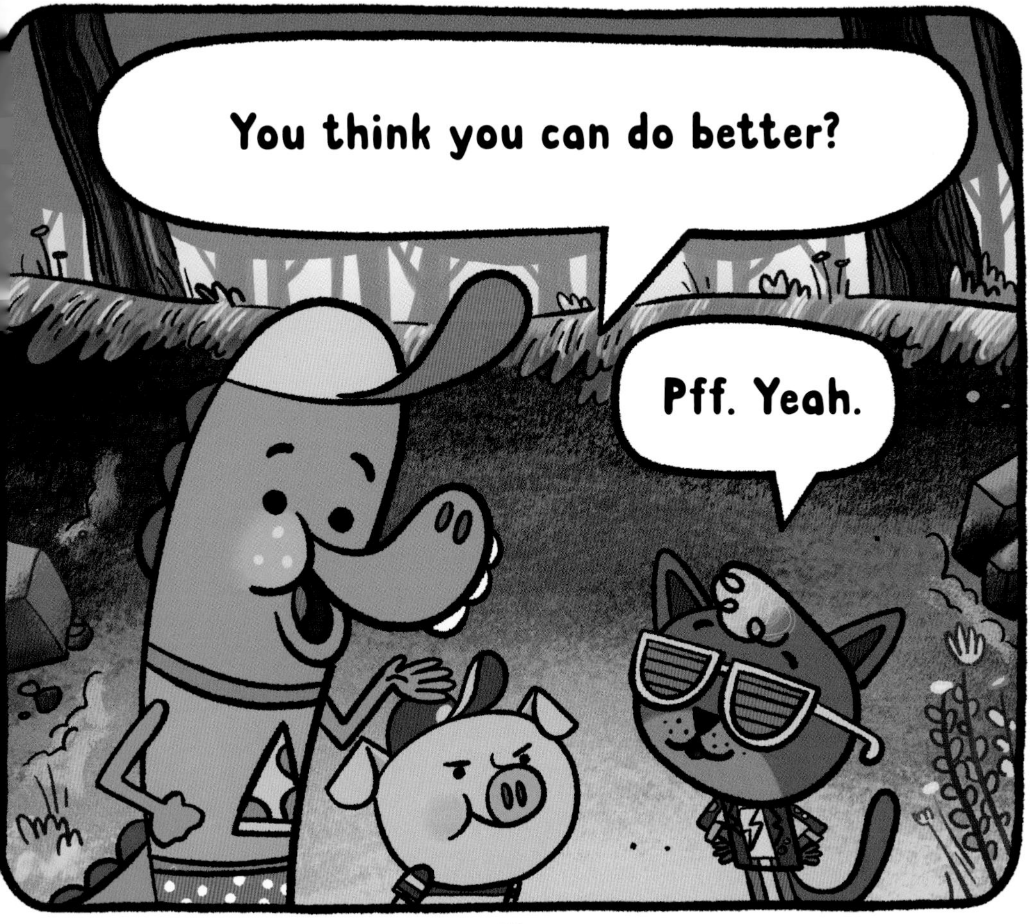
You think you can do better?
Pff. Yeah.

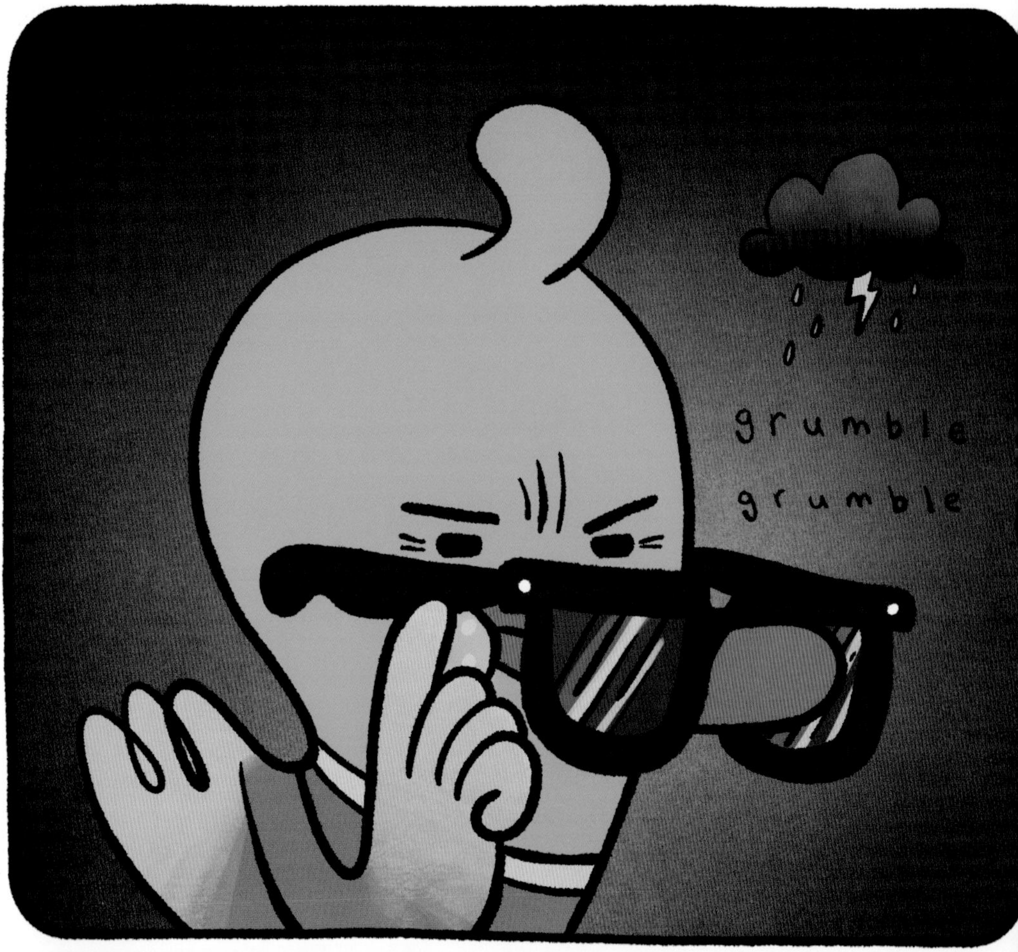
grumble
grumble

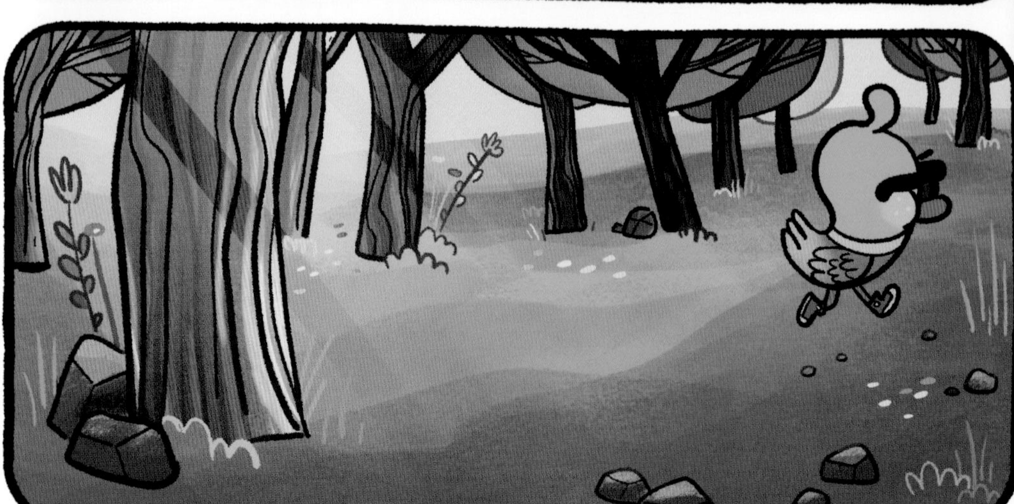

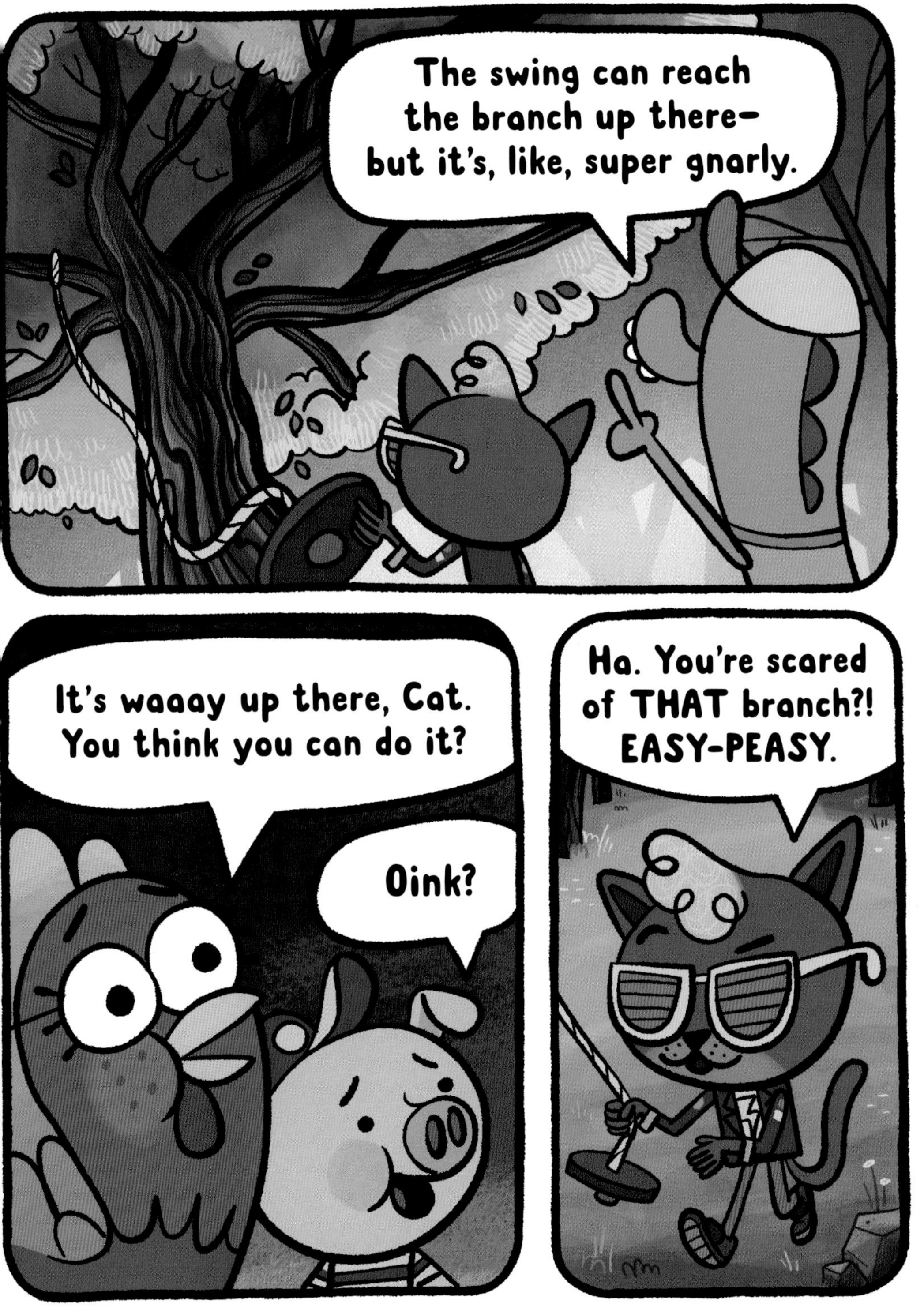
The swing can reach the branch up there—but it's, like, super gnarly.
It's waaay up there, Cat. You think you can do it?
Oink?
Ha. You're scared of THAT branch?! EASY-PEASY.

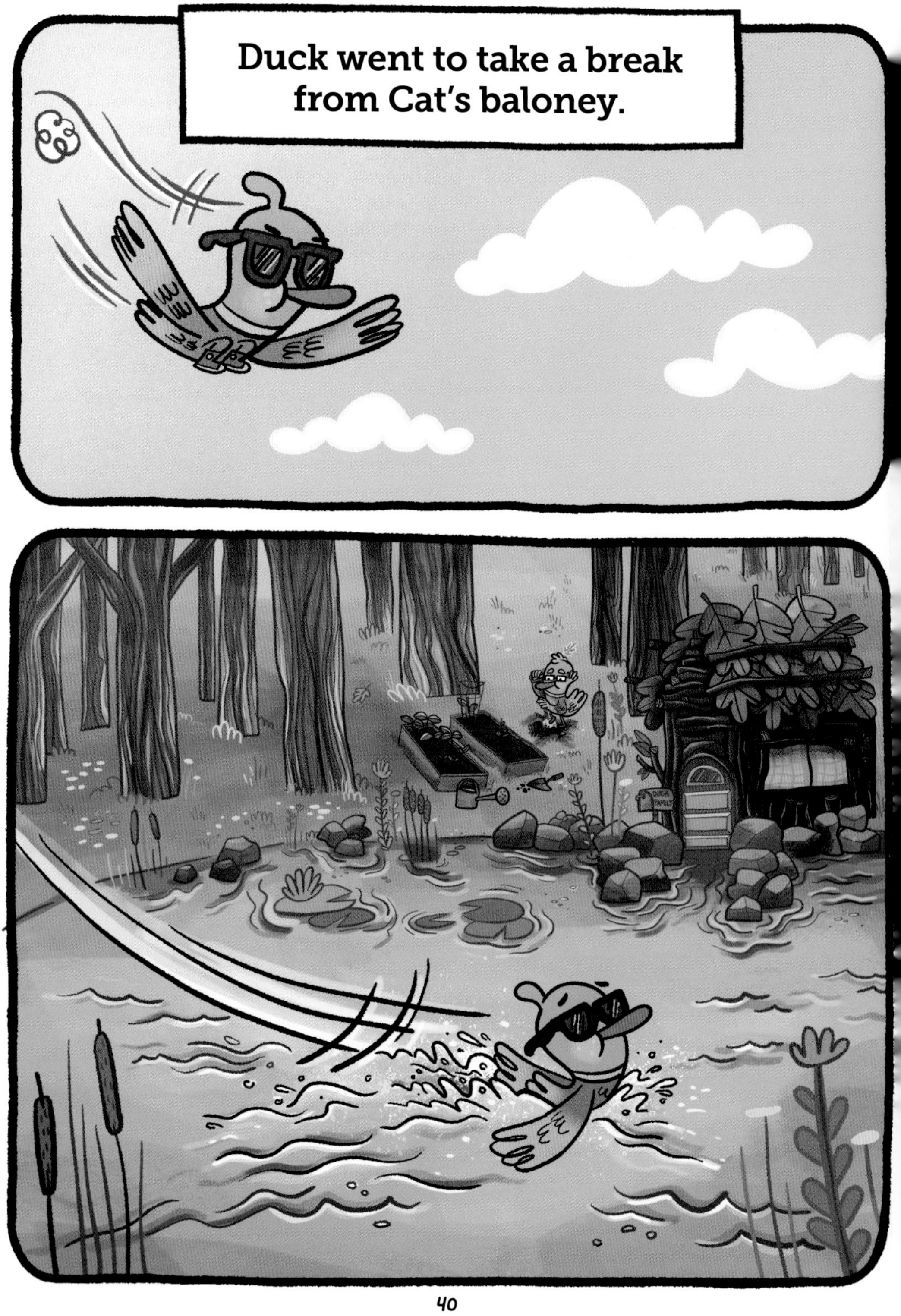
Duck went to take a break from Cat's baloney.

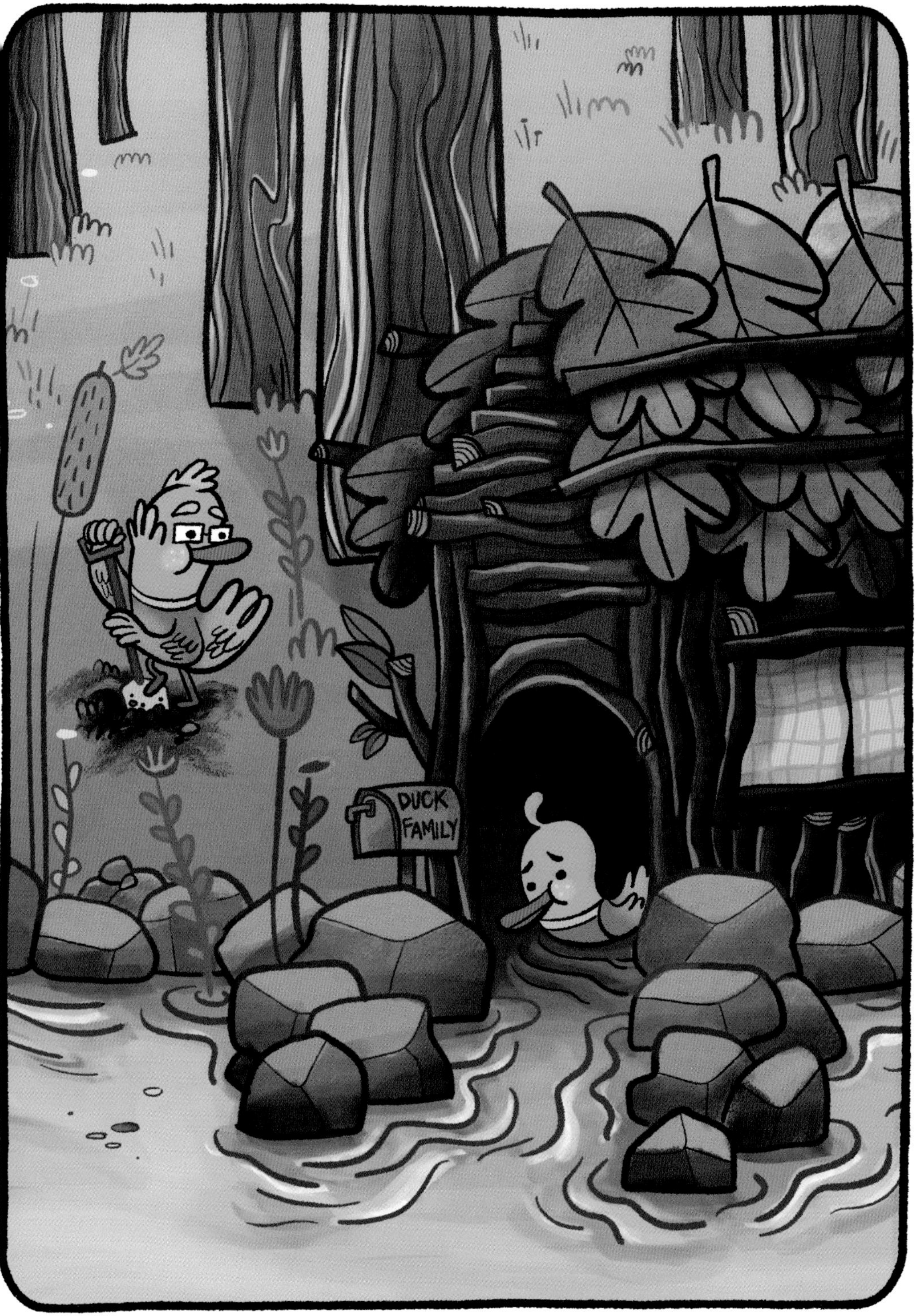
DUCK
FAMILY

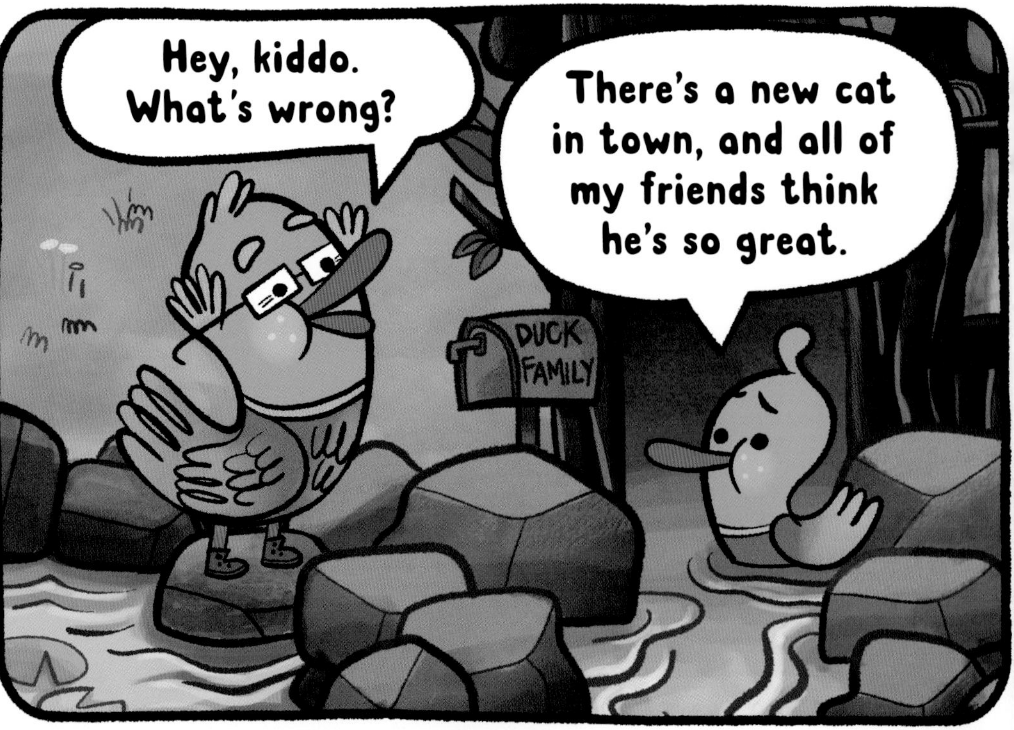
Hey, kiddo. What's wrong?
There's a new cat in town, and all of my friends think he's so great.
DUCK FAMILY

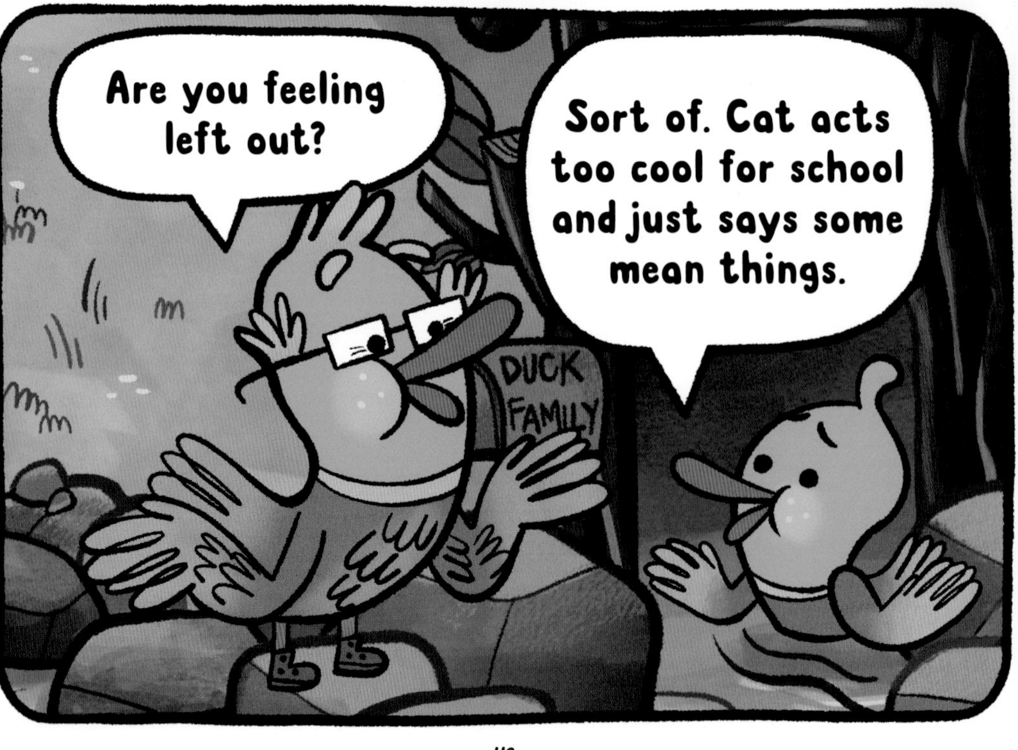
Are you feeling left out?
Sort of. Cat acts too cool for school and just says some mean things.
DUCK FAMILY

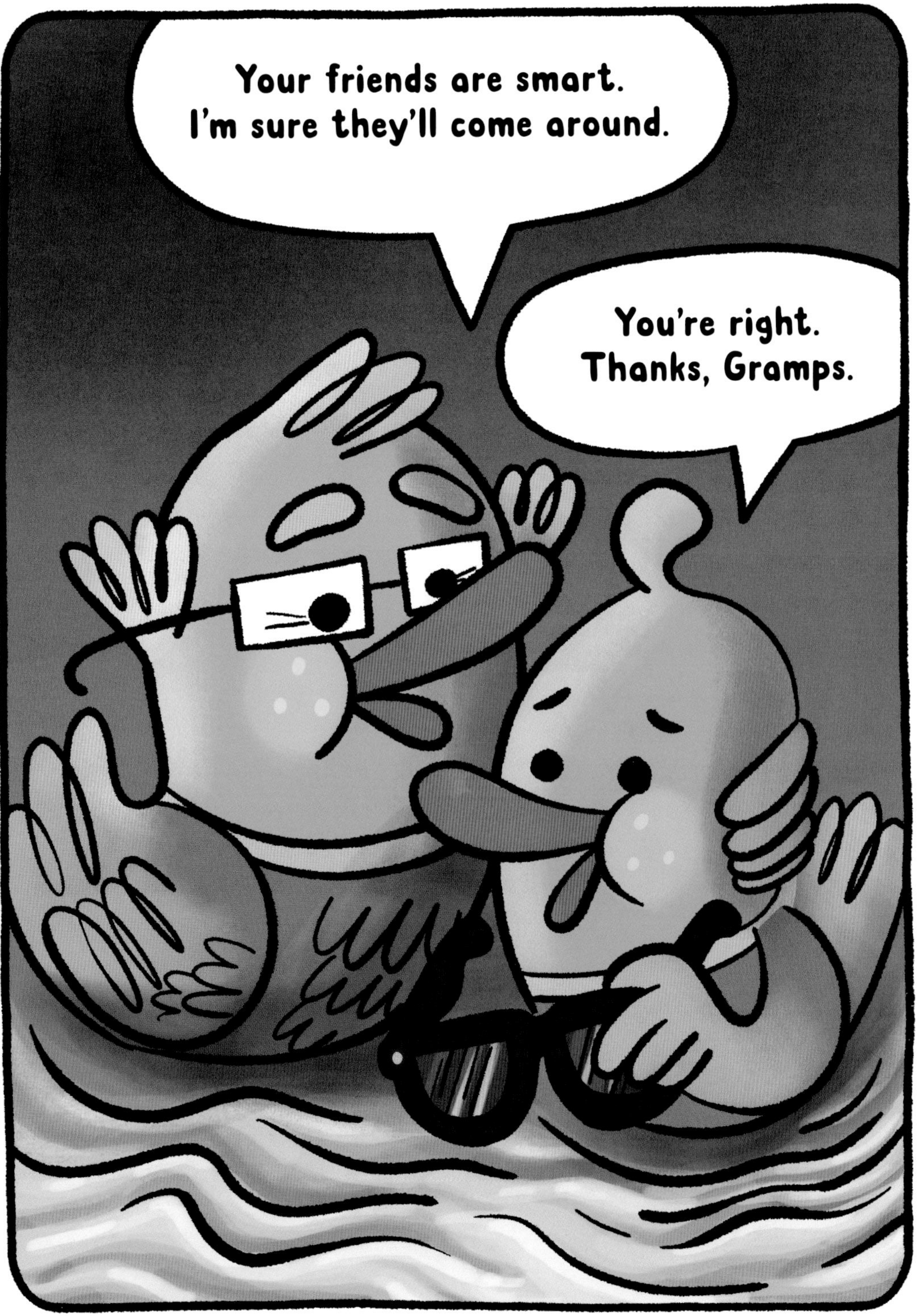
Your friends are smart. I'm sure they'll come around.
You're right. Thanks, Gramps.

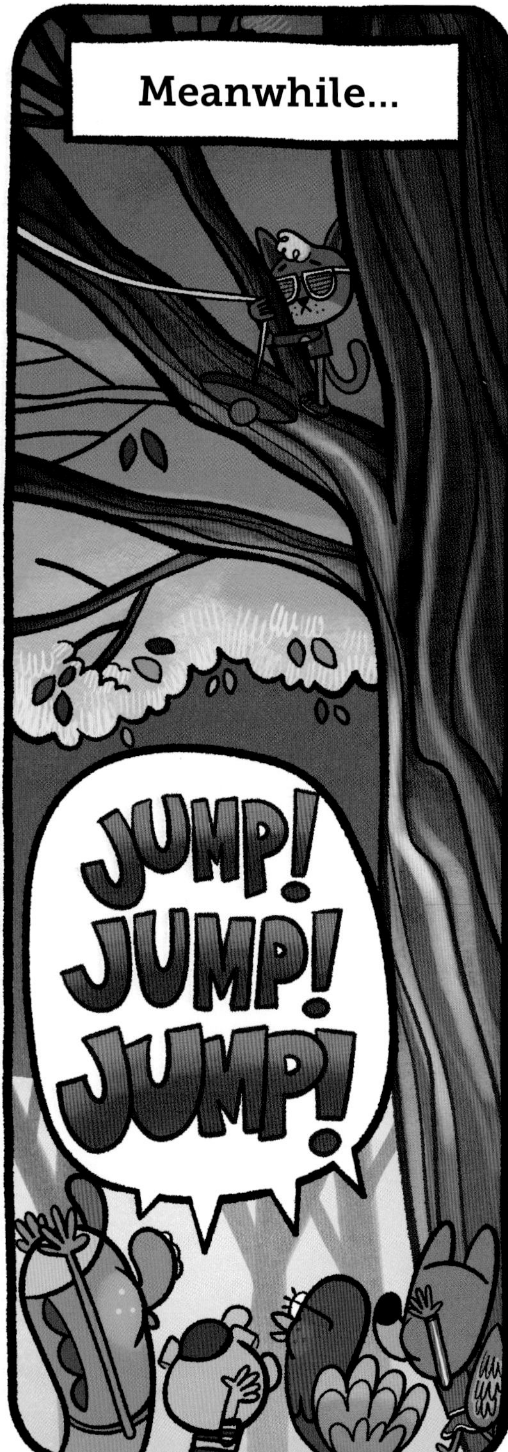
Meanwhile...
JUMP! JUMP! JUMP!

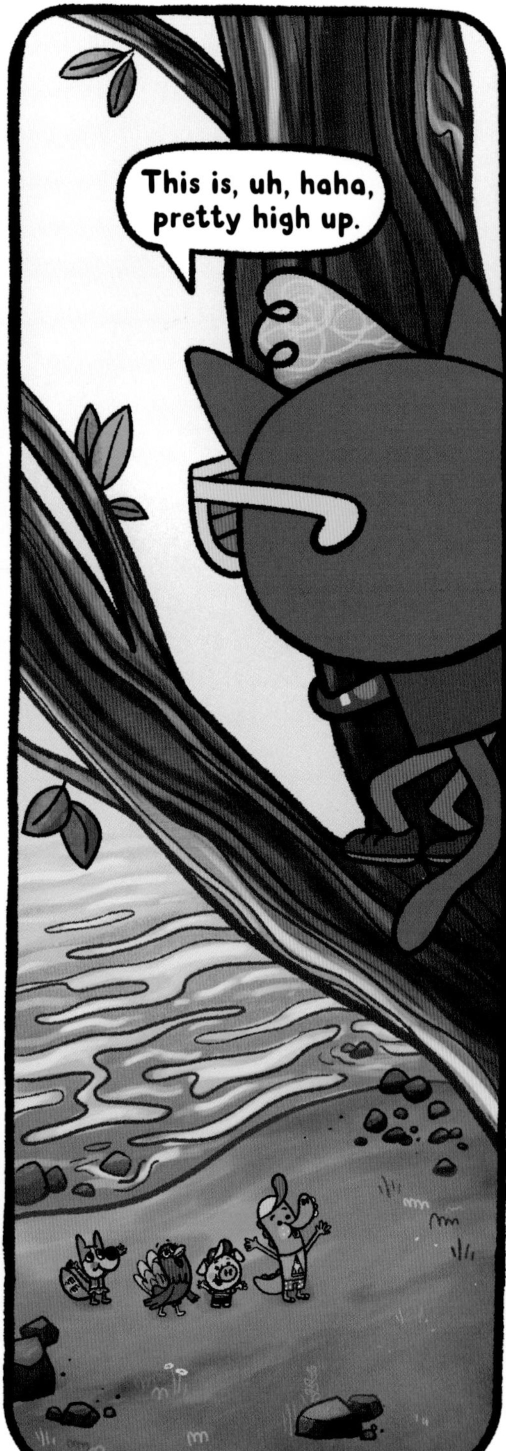
This is, uh, haha, pretty high up.

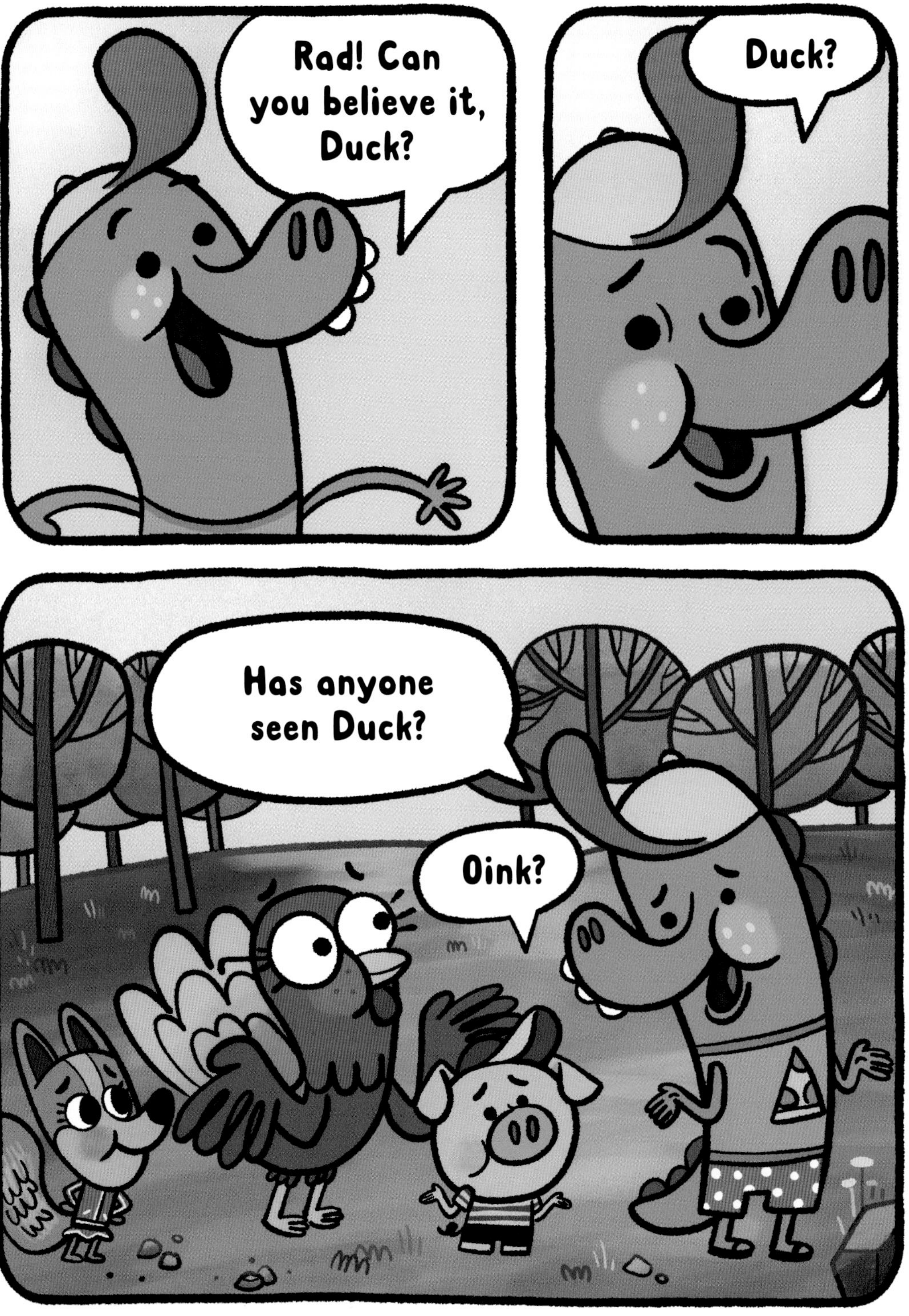
Rad! Can you believe it, Duck?
Duck?
Has anyone seen Duck?
Oink?

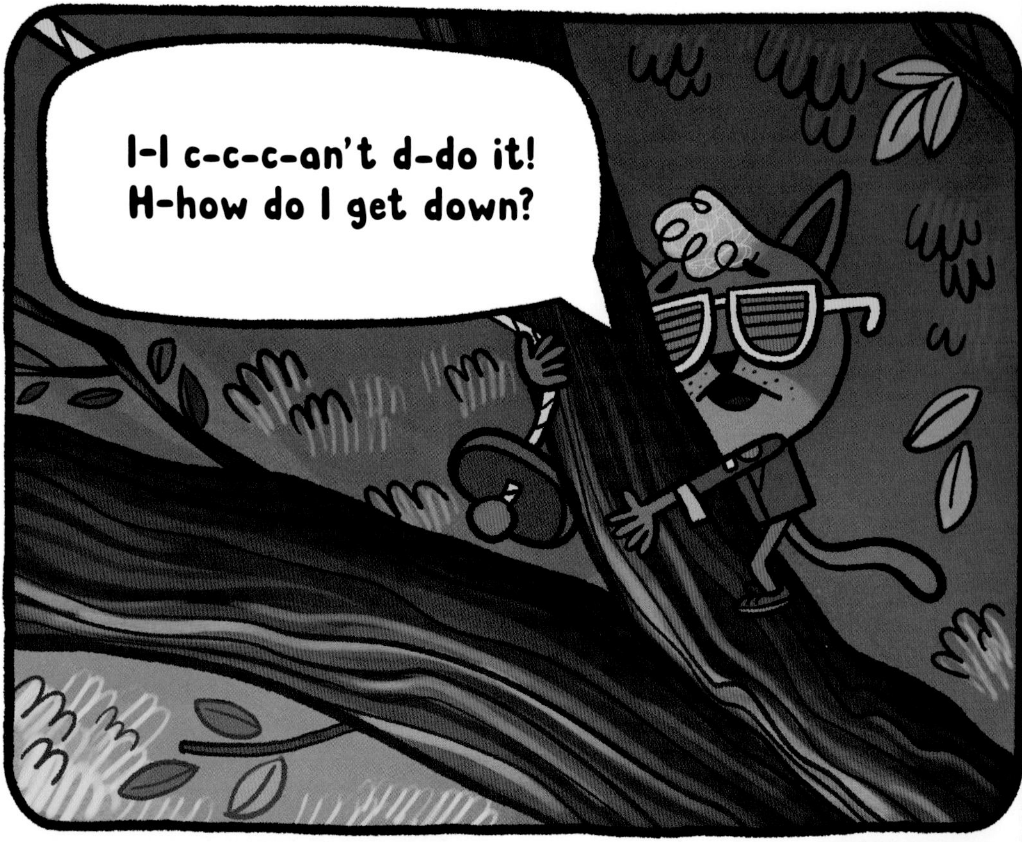
I-I c-c-c-an't d-do it! H-how do I get down?

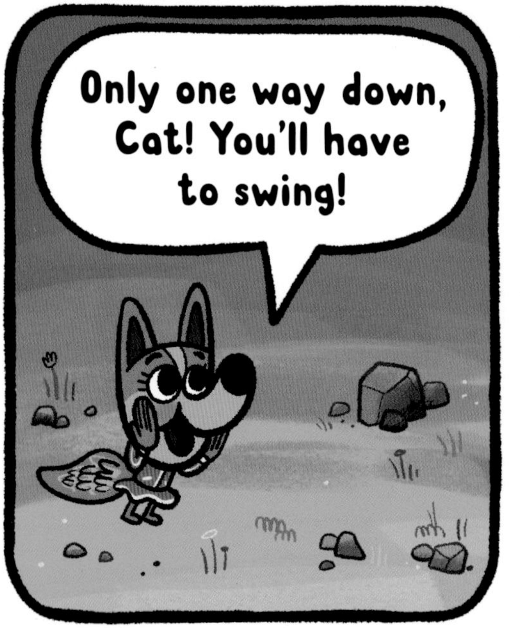
Only one way down, Cat! You'll have to swing!

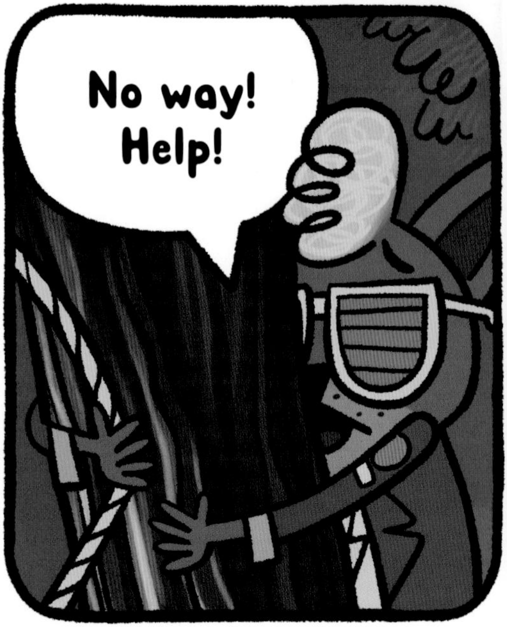
No way! Help!

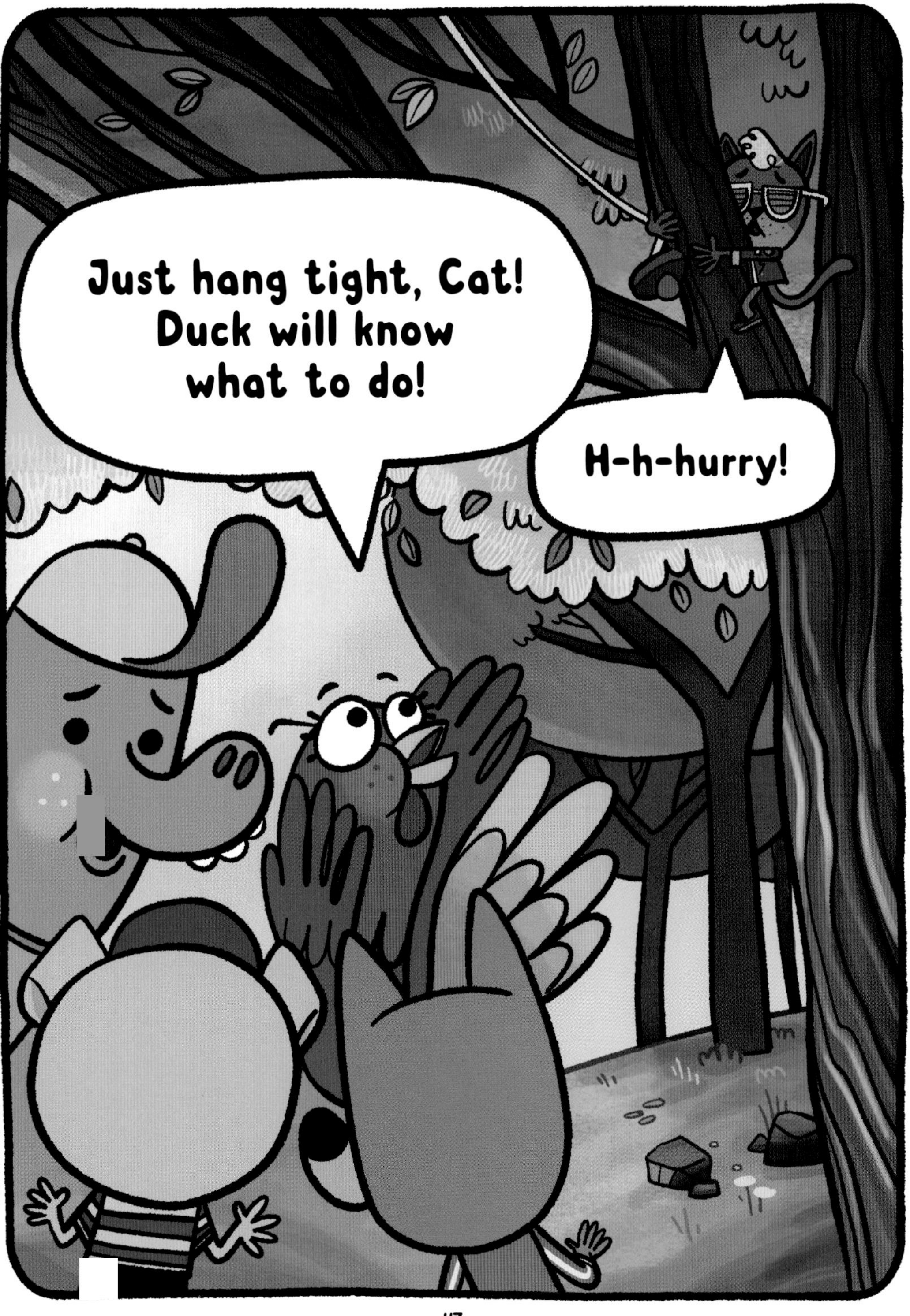
Just hang tight, Cat! Duck will know what to do!
H-h-hurry!

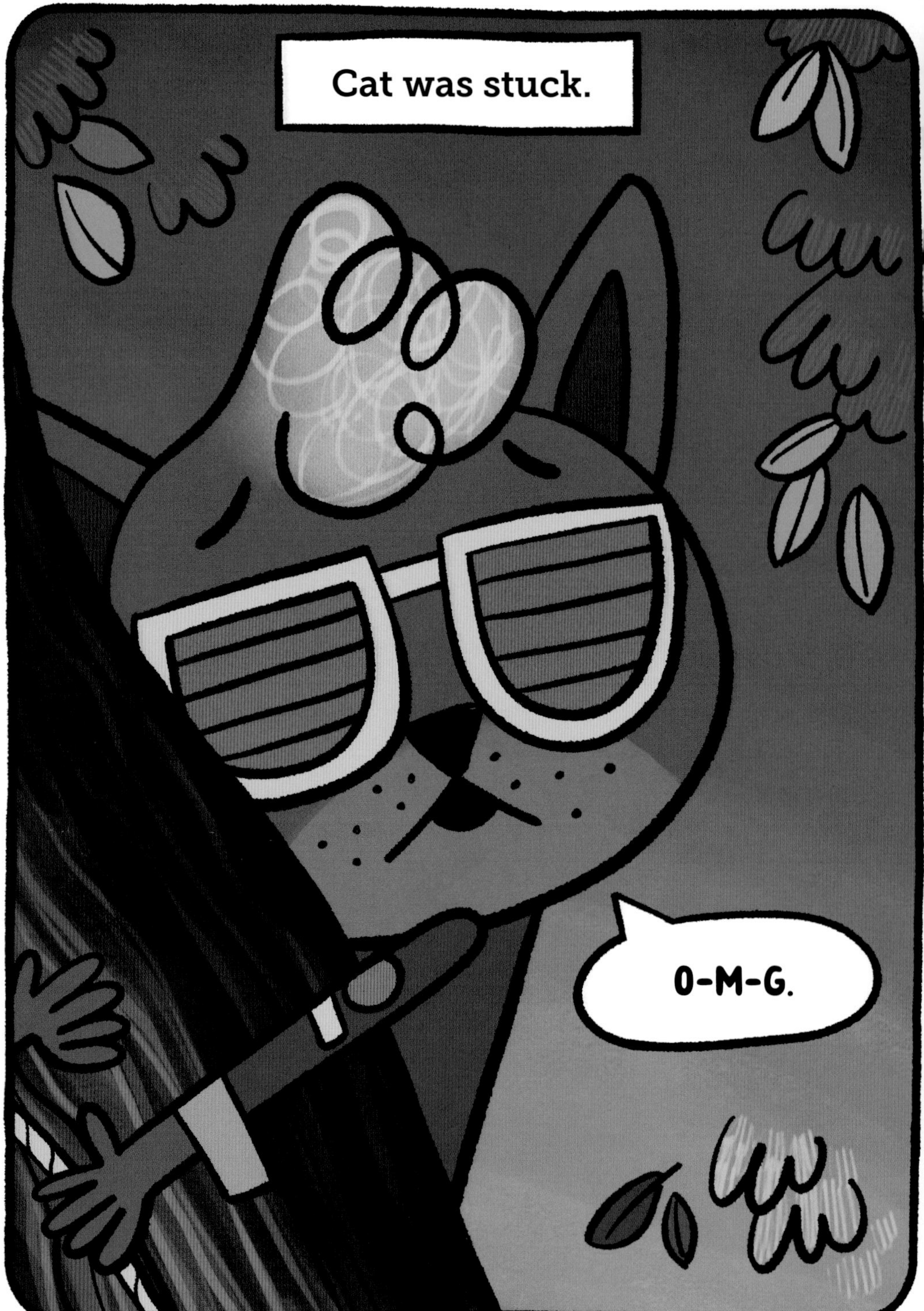
Cat was stuck.
O-M-G.

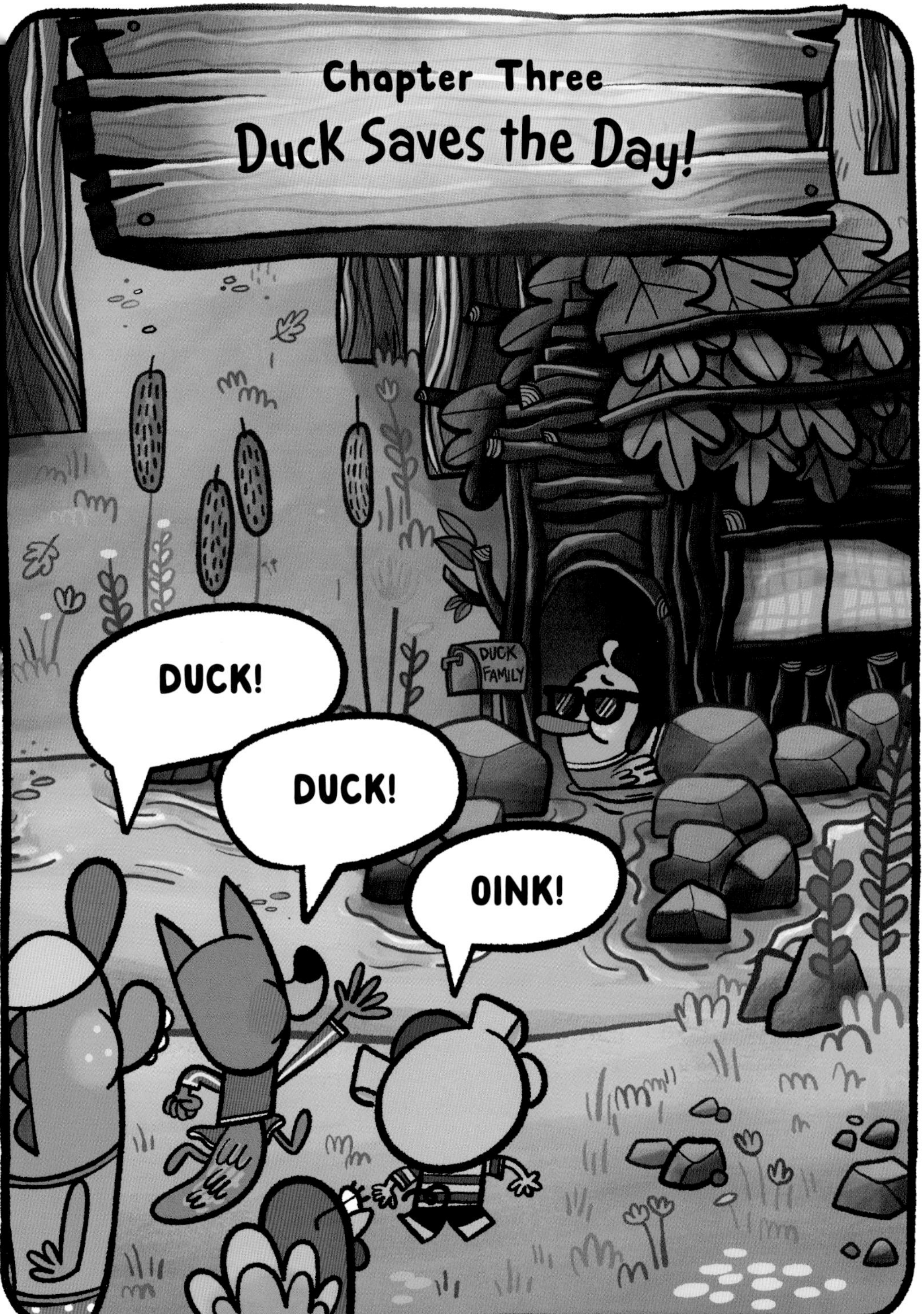

Chapter Three
Duck Saves the Day!
DUCK FAMILY
DUCK!
DUCK!
OINK!

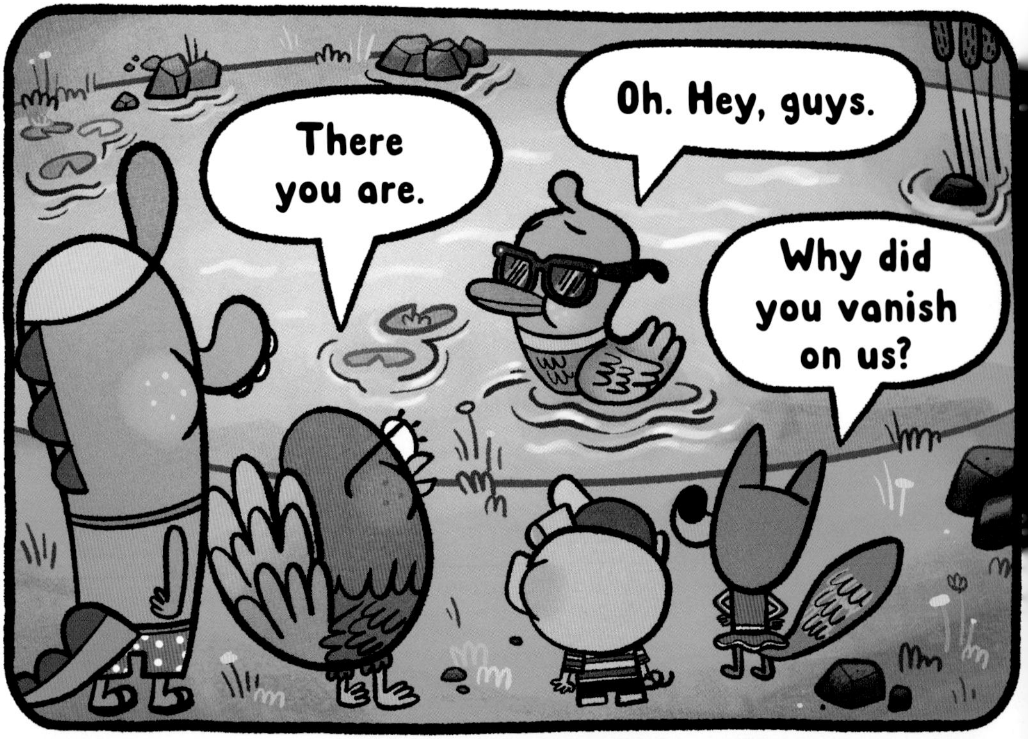
There you are.
Oh. Hey, guys.
Why did you vanish on us?

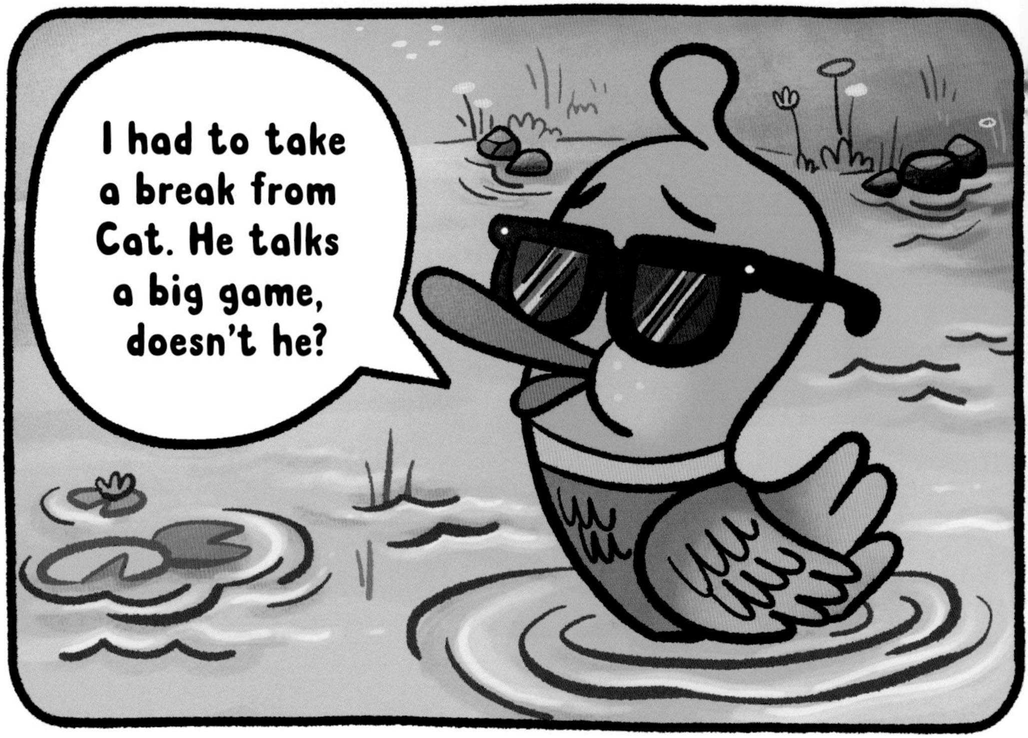
I had to take a break from Cat. He talks a big game, doesn't he?

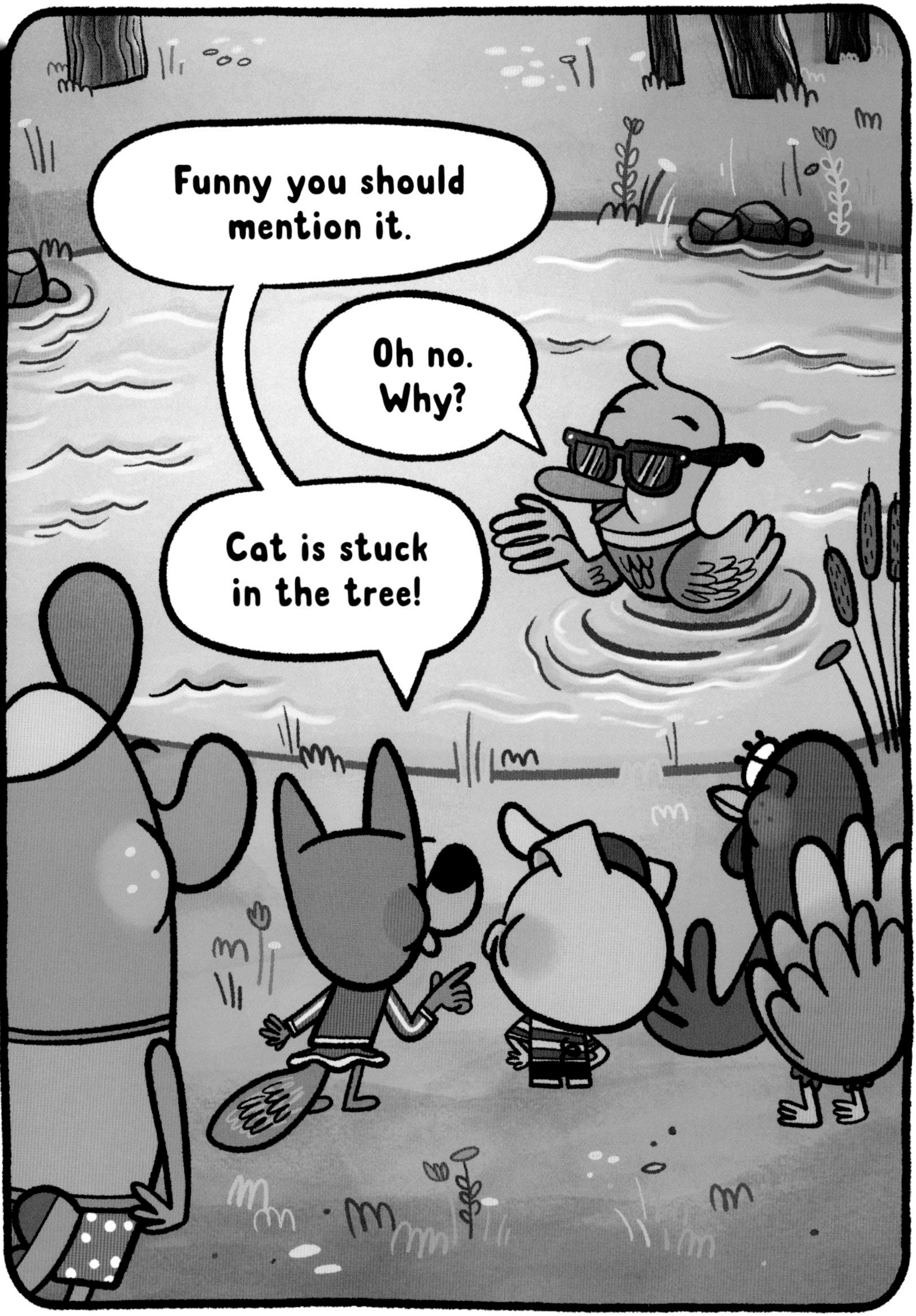
Funny you should mention it.
Oh no. Why?
Cat is stuck in the tree!

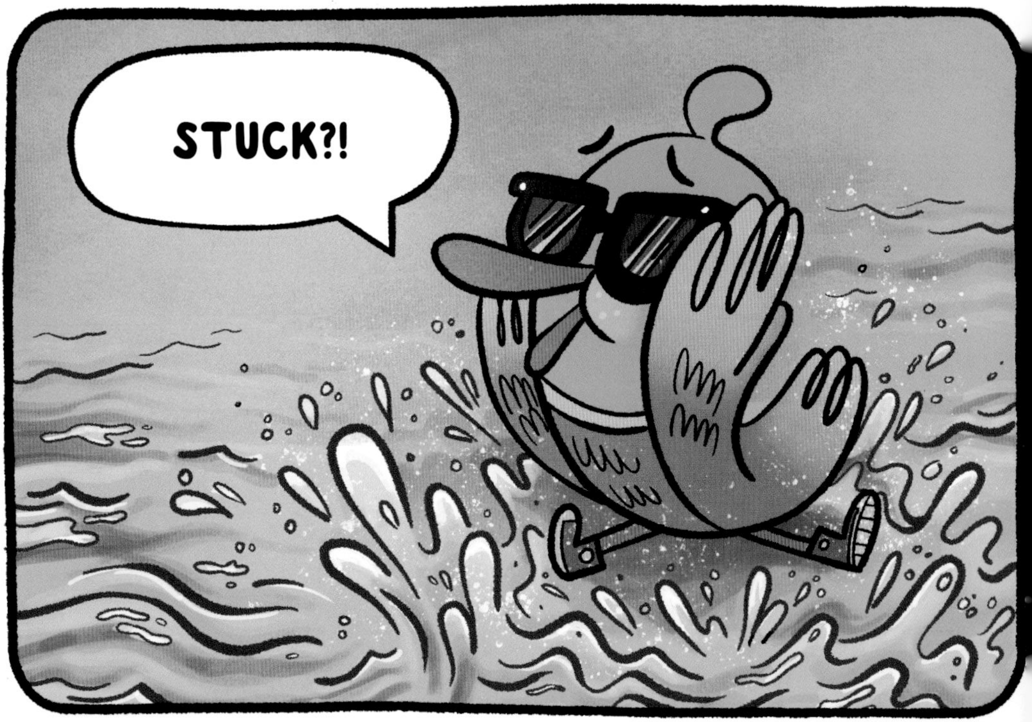
STUCK?!

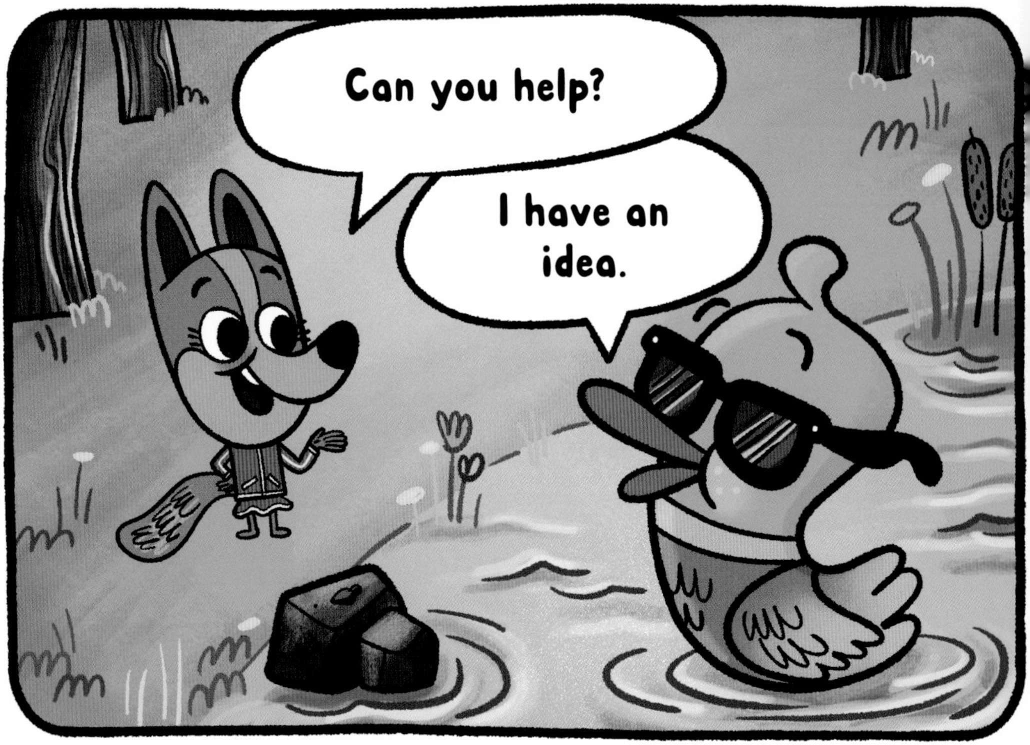
Can you help?
I have an idea.

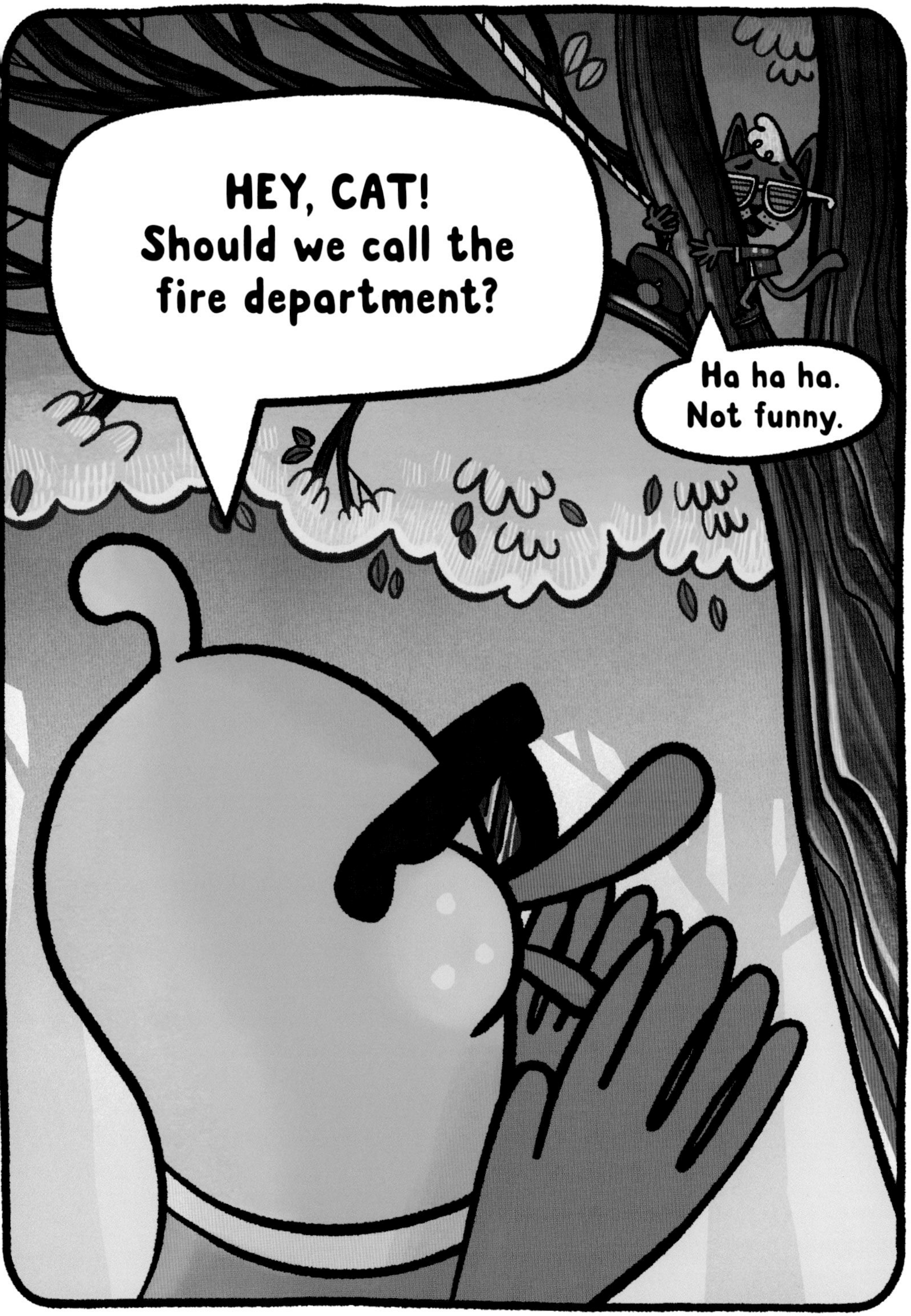
HEY, CAT!
Should we call the fire department?
Ha ha ha. Not funny.

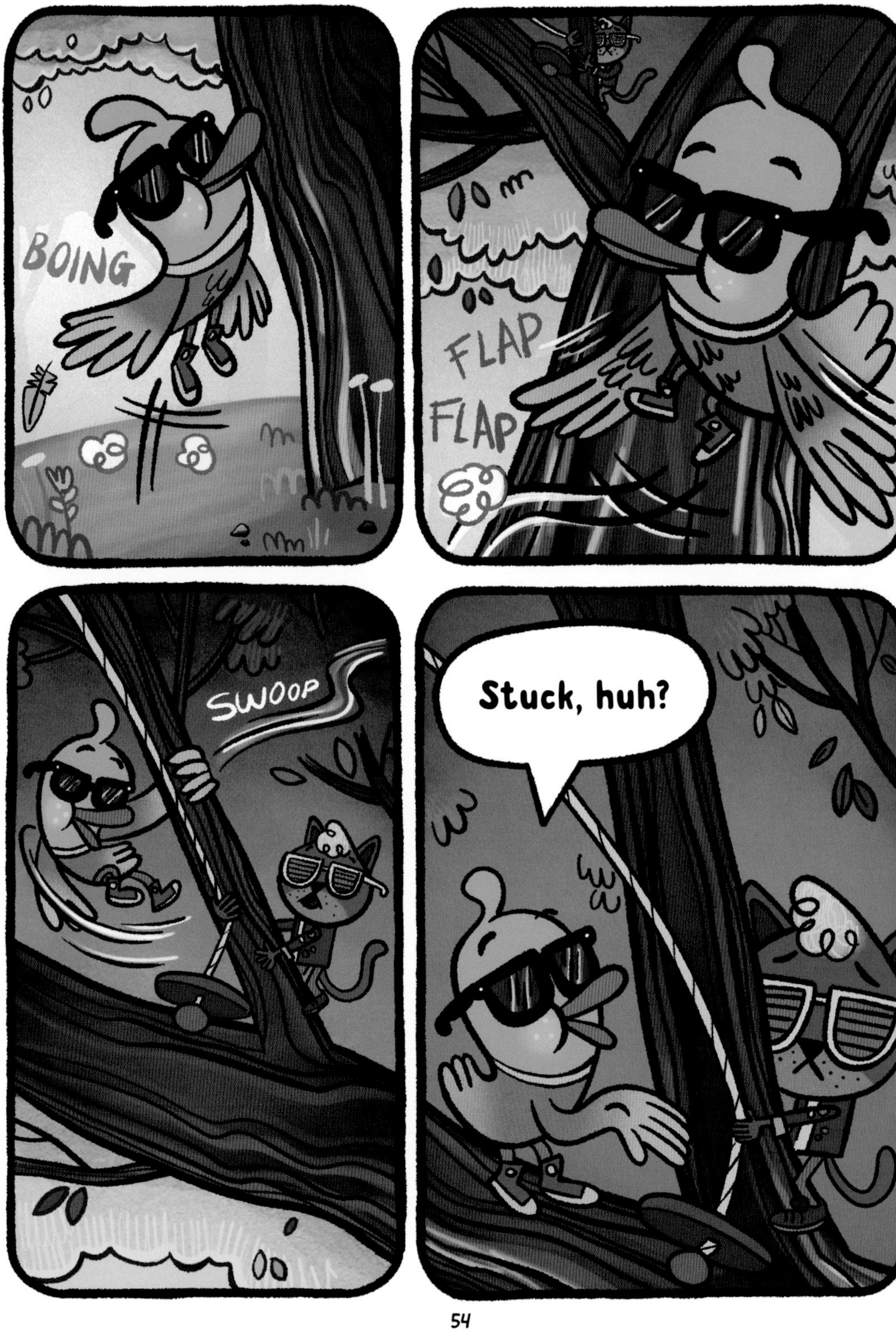
BOING
FLAP
FLAP
SWOOP
Stuck, huh?

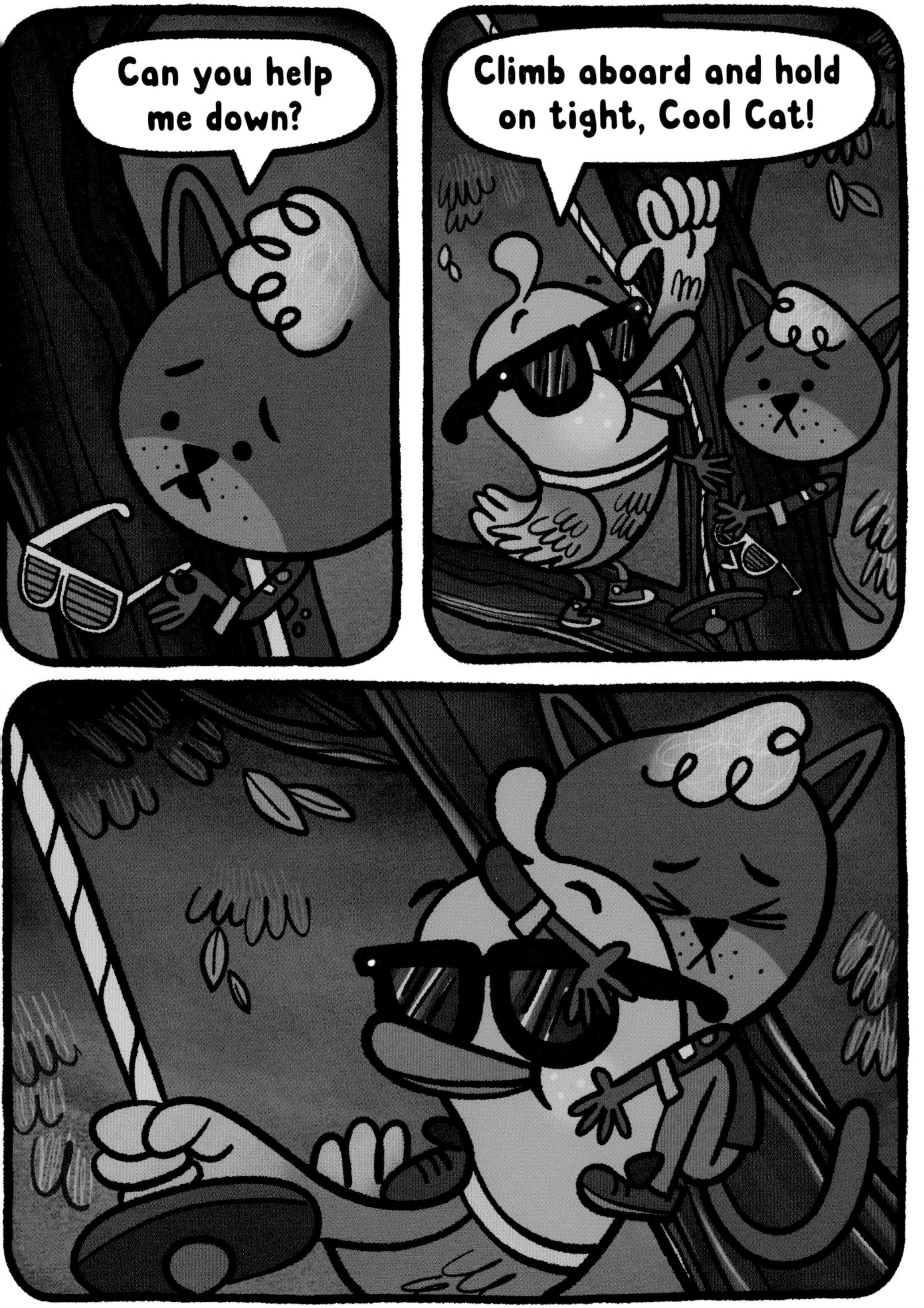
Can you help me down?
Climb aboard and hold on tight, Cool Cat!

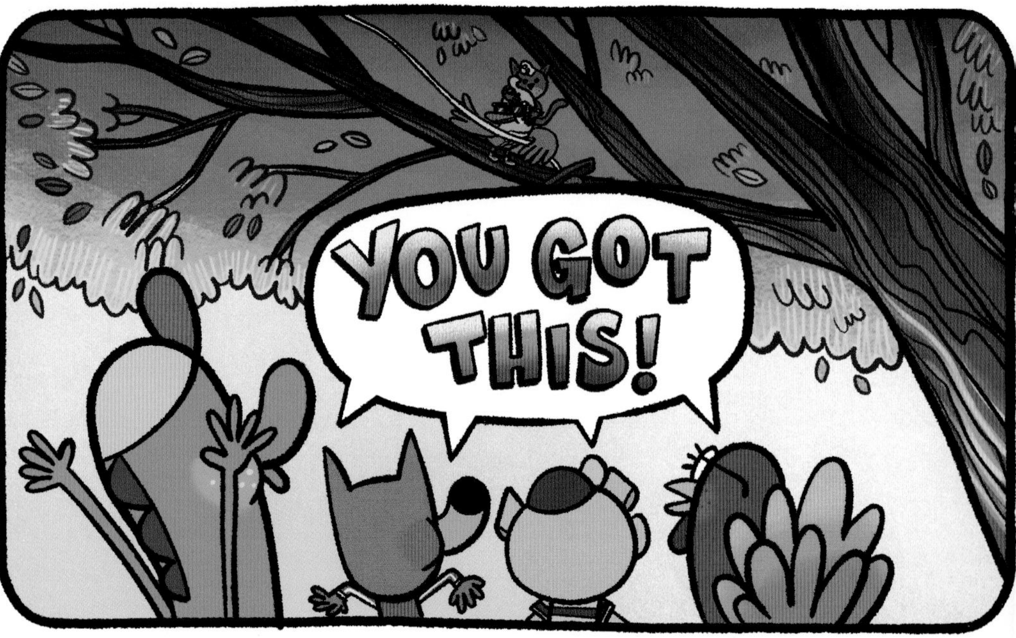
YOU GOT THIS!

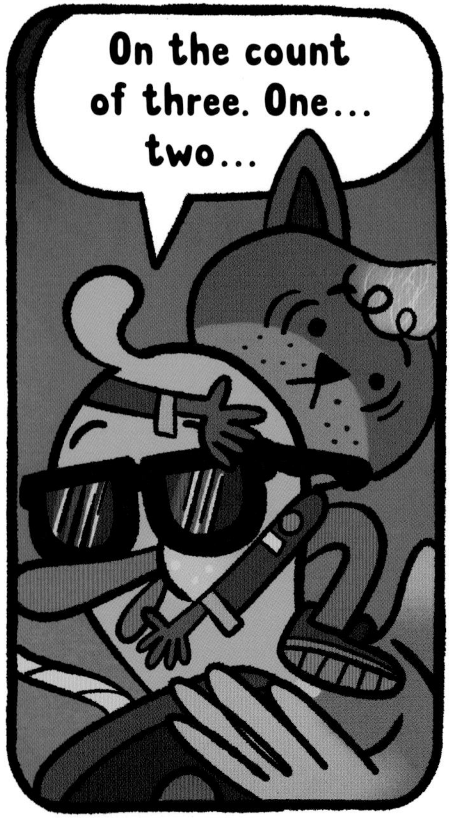
On the count of three. One... two...

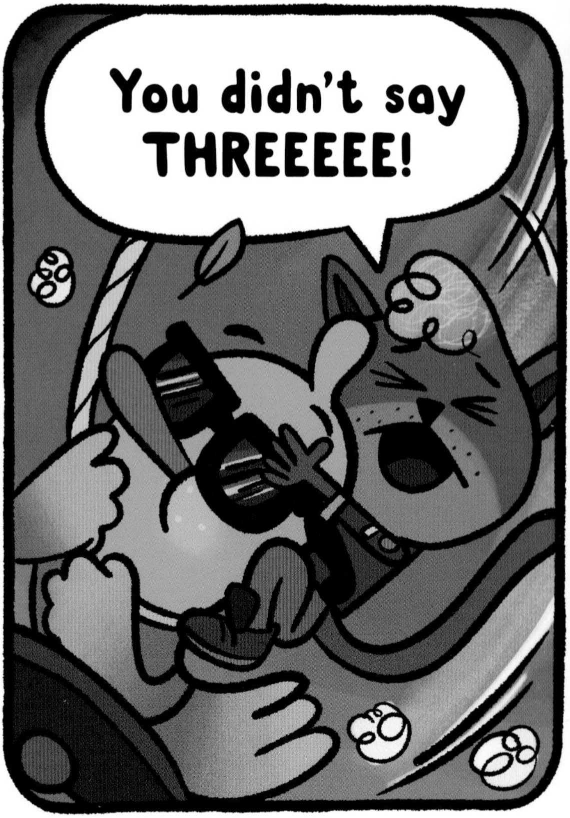
You didn't say THREEEEE!

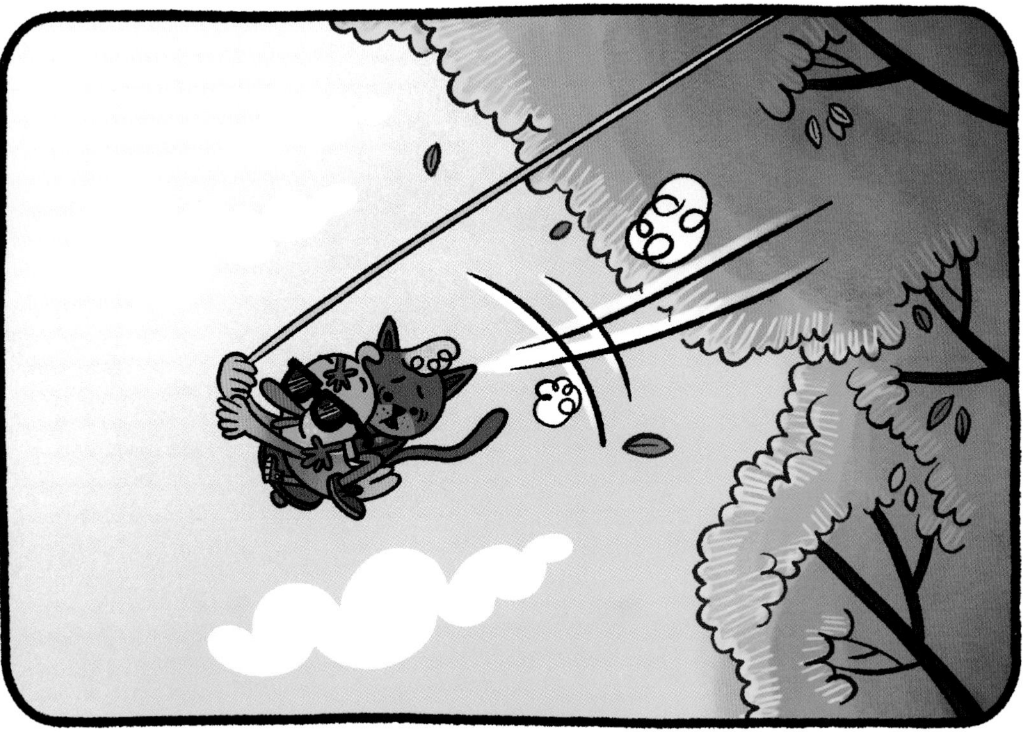

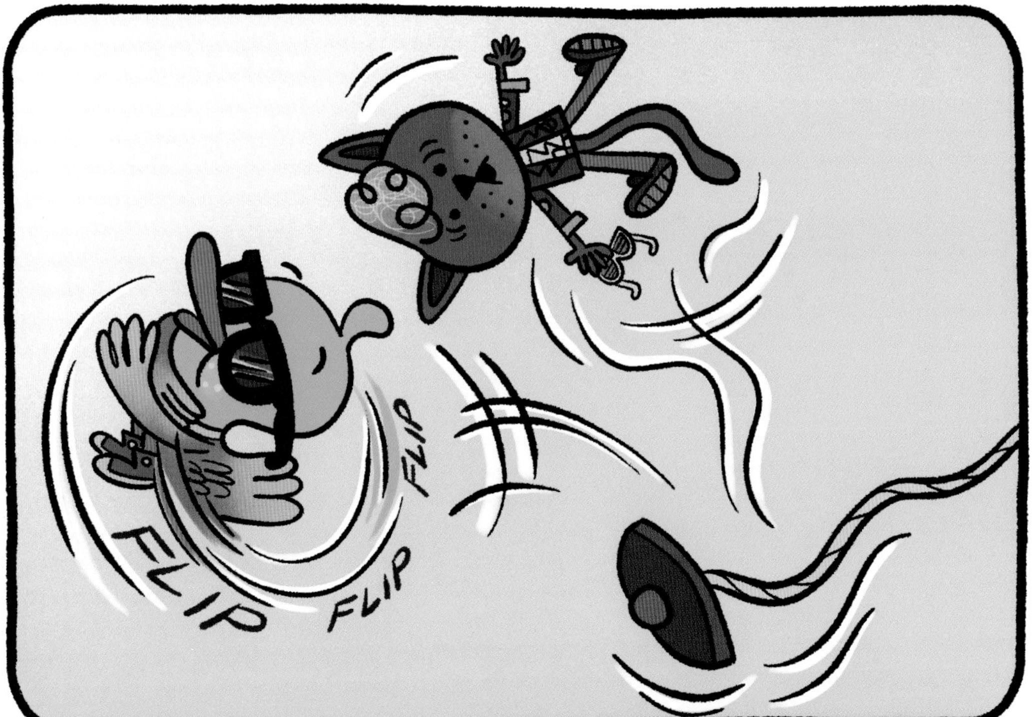
FLIP
FLIP
FLIP

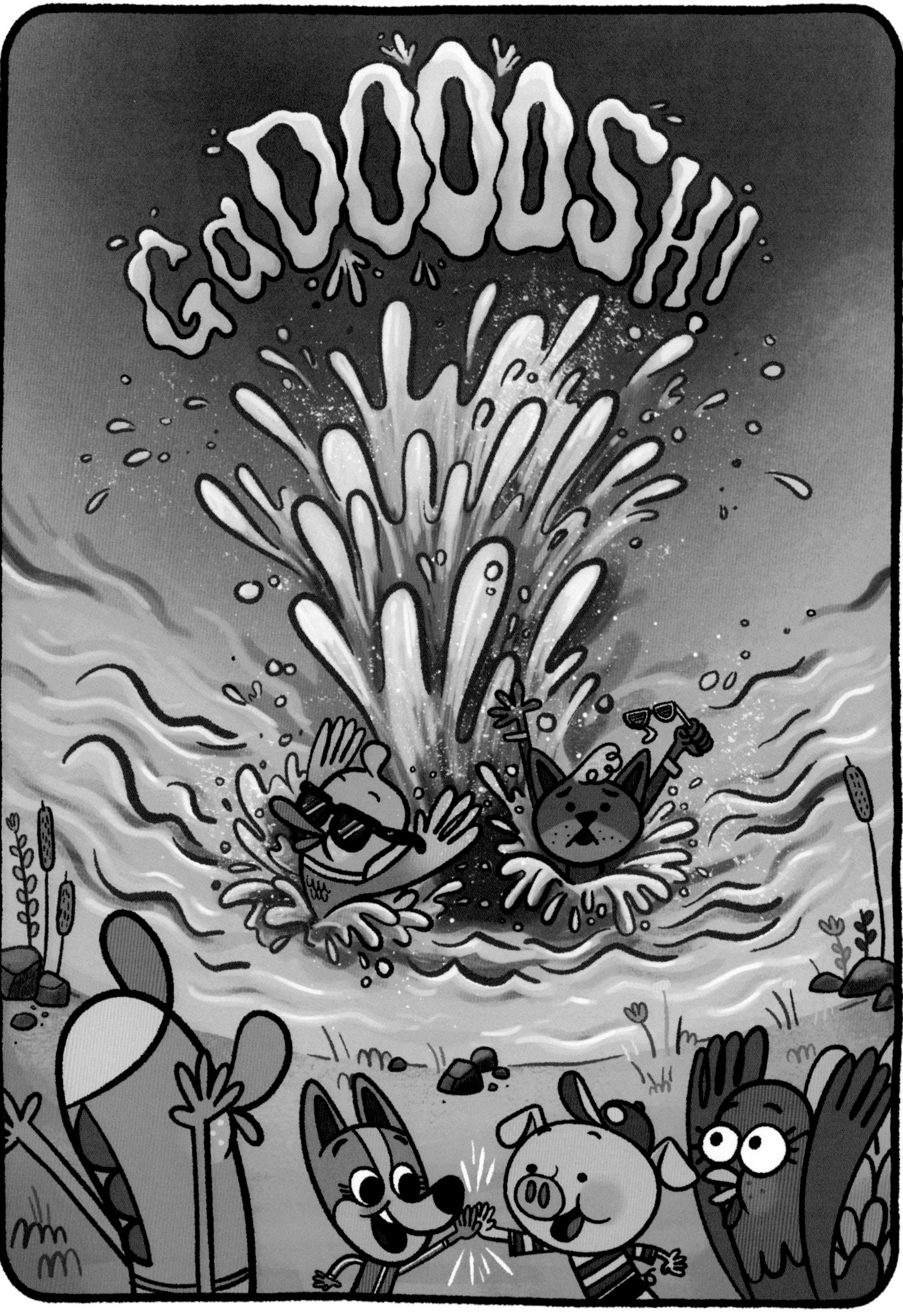
GaDOOOSH!

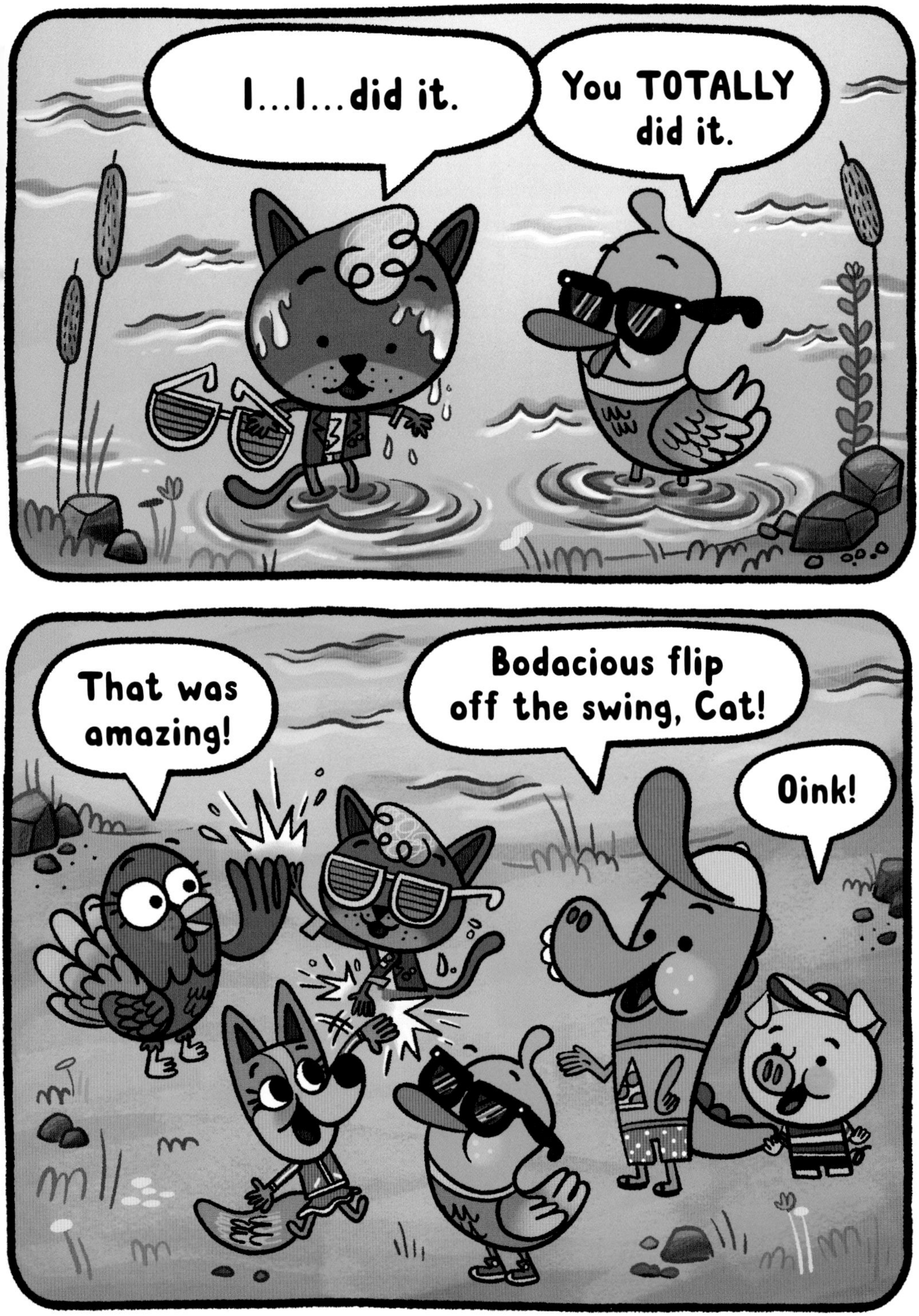
I...I...did it.
You TOTALLY did it.
That was amazing!
Bodacious flip off the swing, Cat!
Oink!

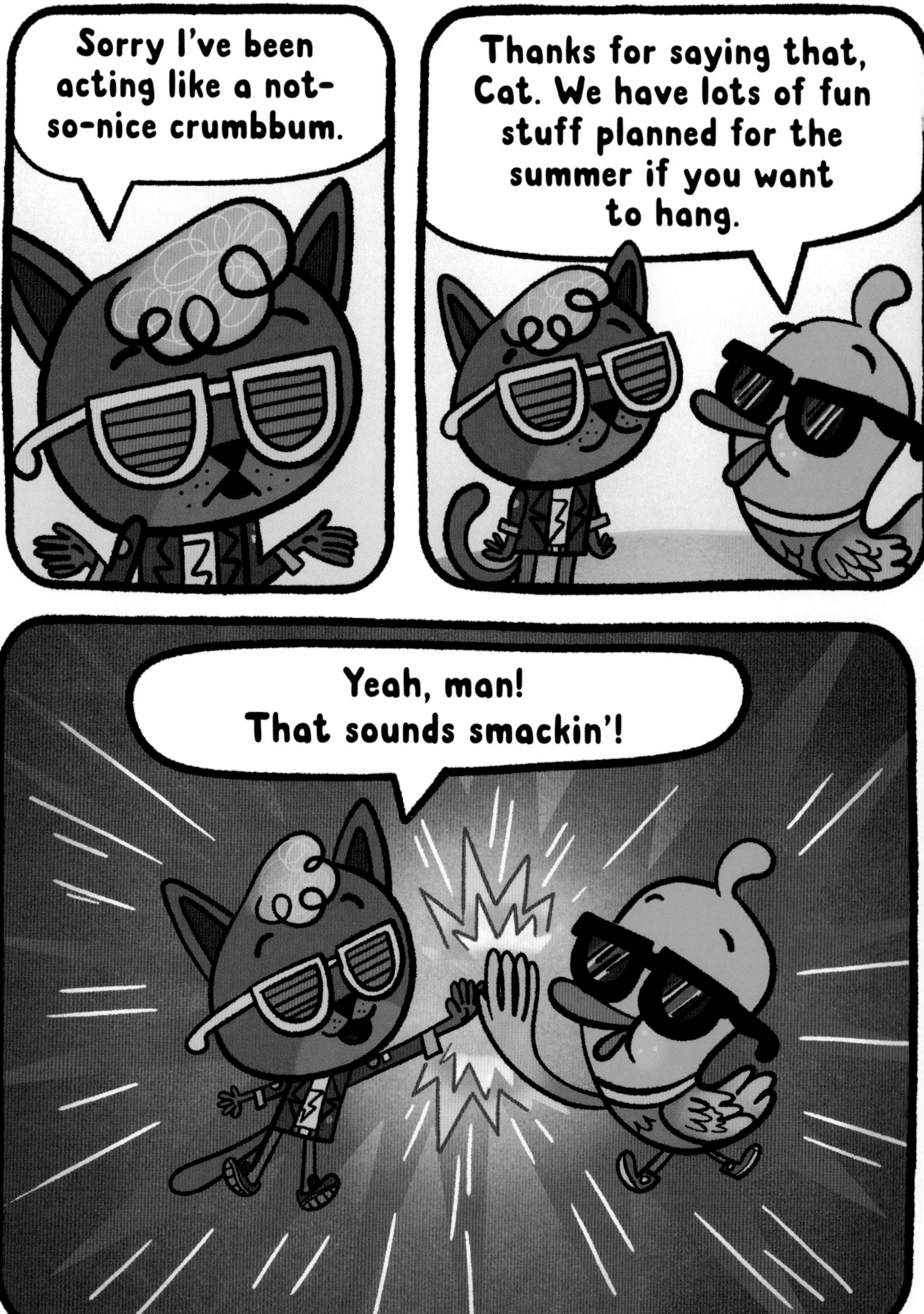
Sorry I've been acting like a not-so-nice crumbbum.
Thanks for saying that, Cat. We have lots of fun stuff planned for the summer if you want to hang.
Yeah, man! That sounds smackin'!

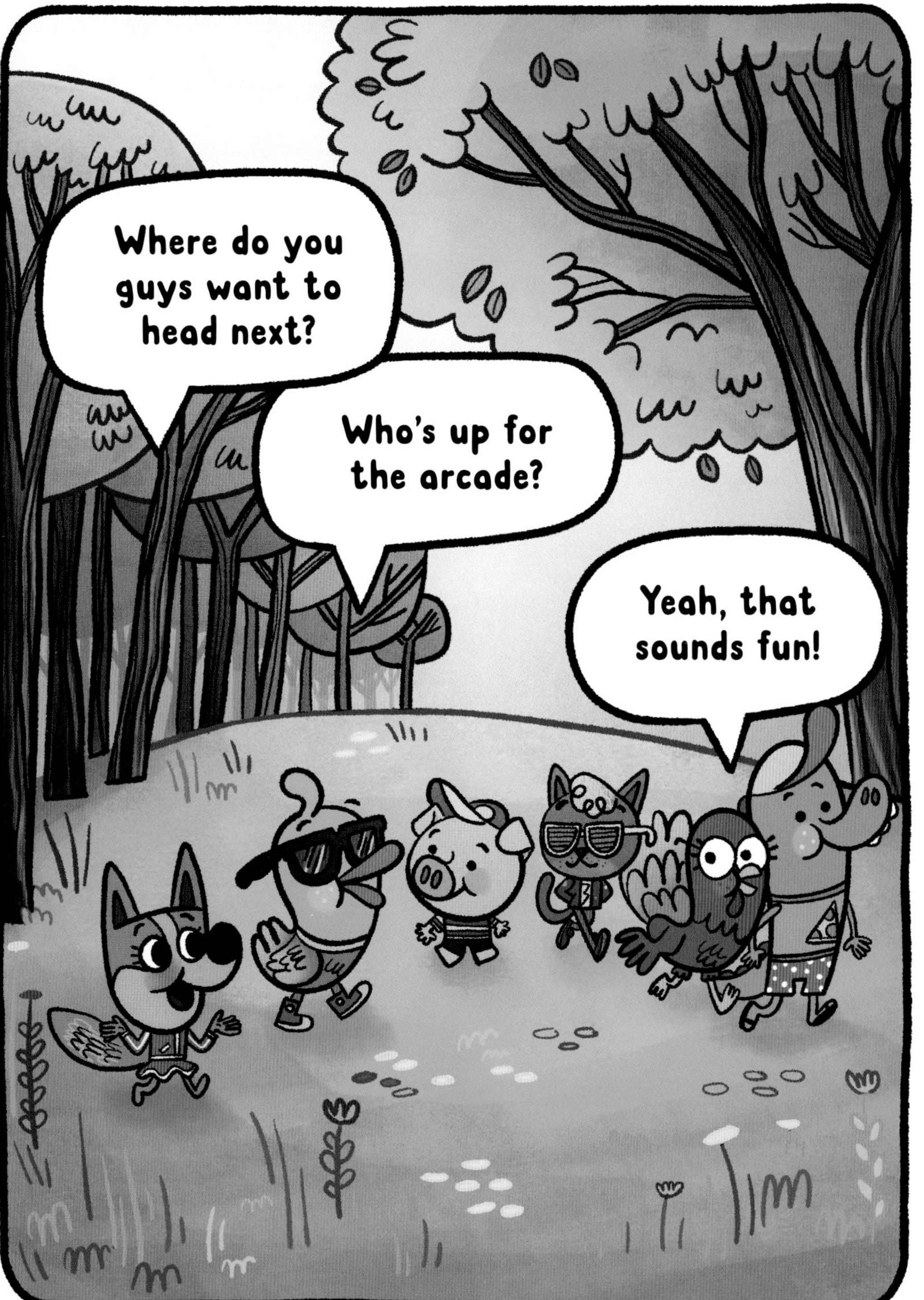
Where do you guys want to head next?
Who's up for the arcade?
Yeah, that sounds fun!

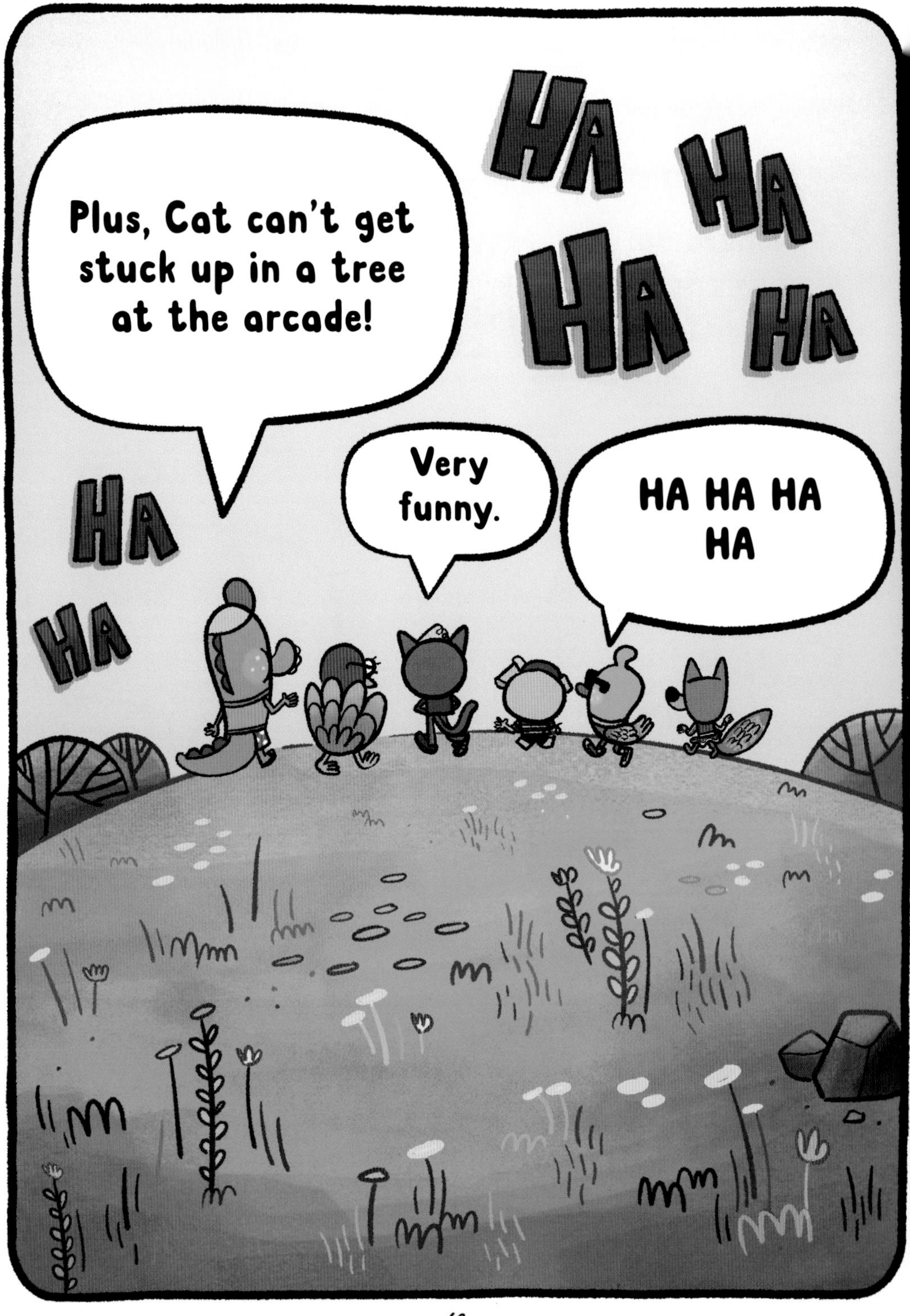
HA HA HA HA
Plus, Cat can't get stuck up in a tree at the arcade!
HA
HA
HA
Very funny.
HA HA HA HA

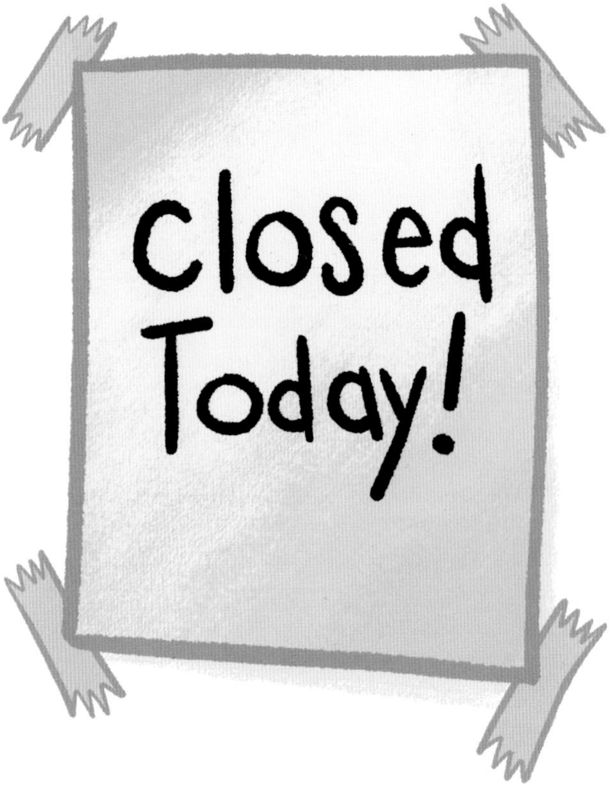
Closed
Today!

The arcade is closed.
The skatepark is jam-packed.
A perfect Saturday with nothing to do!
What will Duck and the gang do
when they have nowhere to hang out?

Find out when you read
One Cool Duck: The Far Out Fort.
Coming soon!

Mike Petrik grew up in the Chicago suburbs shredding on his skateboard, hanging out at the arcade, and just being a cool dude. Mostly, he spent his days drawing. Fast-forward a few years, and Mike has illustrated seven rad picture books (he even wrote one!), created two dynamite lift-the-flap board books, and he can still ollie on his skateboard (although his knees hurt for three days afterward). Mike lives with his stellar wife and three super cool kids in Oak Lawn, IL, and he *loves* a killer slice of pizza. One Cool Duck is his first graphic novel series.

Visit Mike at mikepetrik.com.